HUN

OGILVIE AND THE UPRISING

OGILVIE AND THE UPRISING

Philip McCutchan

Severn House Large Print
London & New York

This first large print edition published in Great Britain 2006 by
SEVERN HOUSE LARGE PRINT BOOKS LTD of
9-15 High Street, Sutton, Surrey, SM1 1DF.
This title first published 2004 by
Severn House Publishers, London and New York.
This first large print edition published in the USA 2006 by
SEVERN HOUSE PUBLISHERS INC., of
595 Madison Avenue, New York, NY 10022.

British Library Cataloguing in Publication Data

McCutchan, Philip, 1920-
    Ogilvie and the uprising. - Large print ed. - (The James Ogilvie series)
    1.   Great Britain. Army - Fiction
    2.   Ogilvie, James (Fictitious character) - Fiction
    3.   India - History - 19th century - Fiction
    4.   Historical fiction
    5.   Large type books
    I.   Title   II. MacNeil, Duncan, 1920-. Matter for the regiment
    823.9'14 [F]

ISBN-10:   0-7278-7497-7

Printed and bound in Great Britain by
MPG Books Ltd, Bodmin, Cornwall.

One

It had started as an overcast day; but a welcome sun pierced the clouds just in time: as Her Majesty Queen Victoria came through the gates of Buckingham Palace past her guard, riding in her great state coach drawn by the Hanoverian horses, accompanied by Her Royal Highness the Princess of Wales and Princess Christian, the day turned bright and auspicious, a perfect setting for the great procession that was to mark Her Majesty's diamond jubilee.

Led by a six-foot-eight officer, Captain Ames of the Life Guards, the long procession rode out for the Wellington Arch, atop which hundreds of loyal subjects were crowded above the flowers and flags, heading for Trafalgar Square amid the cheers and waved bowlers, cloth caps and straw boaters. The occasion was regal in the extreme: some forty princes from all the world marched or rode in the procession – Ferdinand of Bulgaria, Arisugawa of Japan, Mohammed Ali of Egypt, the Amir Khan of Persia, Prince Danilo of Montenegro among them. The Empire, naturally, was strongly represented: the colonial Prime Ministers from Canada and Australia and Natal were accompanied by military units from their own lands – the Natal Mounted Police, the New South Wales Lancers, the Rhodesian Horse. From the Indian princely native states came more than ten thousand soldiers under Lieutenant-Colonel Maharajah Sir Pertab Singh, Regent of Jodhpur, while the British Army in India was represented by B Company of the Queen's Own Royal Strathspey, the 114th Highlanders, under the command of Captain James Ogilvie, trooped home aboard the *Malabar* especially for the occasion and the envy of the rest of the battalion left behind in the Peshawar cantonment.

The bands along the procession played all the military and popular tunes that they knew; the whole air over London seemed to vibrate to the sound of the fifes and drums, the pipes and the brass, and the more muted music of the mounted bands of the Royal Horse Guards and the Life Guards and of the various regiments of dragoons and lancers. Colour and sound was everywhere; never had there been anything like it before. It outshone the golden jubilee as the sun outshone the moon. Queen Victoria was becoming a very old lady, and the people of London in particular were determined to show her that she held a very special place in their hearts. In the clubs that night Her Majesty's health was drunk many times; in the East End the costermongers were out in their pearly suits, and in the music-halls of the capital and in the provinces the jingoistic songs were bawled from lusty throats while tears of pride came to the eyes of the women. The British Empire was at its height and would stay there for ever; and Britain was a splendid place to be. Roared along the Old Kent Road, the words were fitting to the occasion, for uniforms were everywhere:

'We don't want to fight but by jingo if we do,

We've got the ships, we've got the men, we've got the money too...'

There was, in fact, no war in immediate prospect although it was true that Brother Boer looked like getting uppish again and the German Emperor was for ever rattling his sabre, while the Czar of All The Russias was an enigma who was always casting his eyes eastwards. France, too, was going to need slapping down over Fashoda in the Egyptian Sudan; the French had been simmering since 1895, when they had been informed by the British Government that all the Nile valley between the lakes and the southern frontier of Egypt was within the British sphere of influence; but so far the Frogs had done no more than simmer. All the rest was, for the time being at any rate, peace – a fact upon which Colour-Sergeant MacTrease remarked to James Ogilvie when, after the procession had fallen out and the troops had been marched away to barracks, the two were having a drink to-gether. At MacTrease's invitation, the drink was taken in the sergeants' mess at Chelsea Barracks.

MacTrease said, 'The only part o' the army that's fighting is the army in India, sir. That's what I reckon.'

'You've had enough of it, Colour?'

'I didn't mean to say that, sir.' MacTrease took a mouthful of whisky. 'Home service is not for me, and I doubt if I could do with any longer at home than we're getting now.

I'll be glad enough to embark aboard the *Jumna* on Friday week. India gets into a man's blood, sir, do you not find that?'

Ogilvie nodded. 'Yes, I do. Home service would be tame, I fancy. There's a lot we'd miss – even the fighting!'

'Aye.' MacTrease lowered his voice. 'The fighting ... I shouldn't be saying this in someone else's mess, but I have a wee feeling it'd do the Guards, horse and foot, a power o' good to be sent out to the Frontier and learn what's what! Gilded popinjays is what they are, sir, and unless I'm mistaken they've not seen action since the Crimea. But then maybe we'll be finding out for ourselves what they're like, soon.' MacTease paused, somewhat weightily. Then he said, 'I refer to Guardsman Campbell, sir.'

'I thought perhaps you did, Colour. Just between you and me, how do you think it'll work out?'

'It's not for me to say, Captain Ogilvie, sir.'

'Oh, come on!' Ogilvie grinned. 'I said, it's between you and me. Don't be a shy floweret, Colour!'

'That'll be the bloody day, sir.' MacTrease drank more whisky and wiped the back of a hand across his mouth. 'I don't really know, sir, and that's the truth. Gentlemen rankers are a funny lot, sir. They join for one of two reasons: either they're determined to get a commission, and I say good luck to the buggers if they can make it. Or they're drunkards or such, gentlemen who've been thrown out by their families in disgrace for one thing or another – drink as I said, or women, or cards, or even crime. The army's all that's left – for gentlemen.'

'The second category doesn't include Guardsman Campbell, Colour.'

'No, sir, I understand not. I understand he wishes to make a career of the army, so he'll pull his weight. Just the same, there are points against him. I believe he's asked for a transfer simply because he's not made lance as soon as he should if he wants to be considered for a commission. Not because he wants to join *us*. It looks like he's having a second attempt as it were ... and that doesn't strike me as too bloody bright, sir.'

'There's the other side of the coin, Colour.'

MacTrease frowned. 'Sir?'

'He may want to see some foreign service. He may agree with you about gilded popinjays!'

'Aye, sir.' MacTrease gave a short laugh.

'Maybe so, and we'll be finding out. But I'll tell you something else, sir: the Jocks won't like it over much. The soldiers never like the gentlemen rankers and they can make life hell if they decide to, sir.'

'Well, I hope they won't, Colour, that's all. He's to be given his chance. Surely there's one thing already in his favour, isn't there?'

'What's that, sir?'

'He's a Scot!'

Once again MacTrease gave his short laugh, a harsh and humourless sound. 'Aye! As a Scot, why didn't he join a Scots regiment from the start, Captain Ogilvie?'

Next morning, James Ogilvie had a job to do and it concerned Guardsman Campbell of the Coldstream. Back in India he had been asked by Lord Dornoch, his Colonel, to interview Campbell whilst in London, and if in his view the young soldier appeared suitable to serve in the Royal Strathspey he would be drafted to the depot at Invermore for kitting-out and induction into the ways of a Highland regiment before being sent to join the battalion on the North-West Frontier – this was, if the GOC London District should approve the transfer, which he no doubt would if neither the CO of the Coldstream battalion nor the officer commanding the Royal Strathspey found objections. Upon his arrival in London Ogilvie had formally approached the Coldstream adjutant by letter, and the interview had been arranged for the morning after Her Majesty's jubilee procession.

Ogilvie presented himself, in uniform, at Wellington Barracks shortly before the appointed time and was taken in hand by the Adjutant. Expecting strict formality from Her Majesty's Foot Guards, he was taken aback by the extent of it when he entered the orderly room. Present beside himself and the Adjutant were Campbell's Company Commander, the Regimental Sergeant-Major, and the Colour-Sergeant of Campbell's company, all looking like ramrods in their scarlet tunics and forage caps with the edges of the peaks gilded and pulled down over their noses so that they had to hold their heads back to see at all. The Adjutant stood with Ogilvie behind a plain wooden table; at his nod the Regimental Sergeant-Major vibrated in a salute, yelled: 'Sir!' and then stalked to the door which was flung open for him by a lance-corporal who stared woodenly at his front. At the doorway the Regimental Sergeant-Major, standing

12

rigid with his cane beneath his arm, halted and delivered his vocal broadside.

'Guardsman Campbell! Quick – *march*! Left, right, left, head up, man, keep your *shoulders* back! Left, right ... *'alt!'* The RSM slammed to the salute once more and somewhat unnecessarily announced in a bellow, 'Sir! Guardsman Campbell, sir, special request, to see Captain Ogilvie of the 114th Highlanders. Sir!'

'Thank you, Sar'nt-Major,' the Adjutant said. There was another salute that swept the air like a fan. 'Stand the man at ease, if you please.'

The order was screamed out and Campbell's legs sprang apart while his hands seemed to click into place behind his back. Like the lance-corporal he stared into space, army fashion, a little over the top of Ogilvie's head: officers must not be stared at directly. Ogilvie glanced aside and caught the Adjutant's eye. The Adjutant said, 'All yours, Captain Ogilvie.'

'Thank you.' Ogilvie looked Campbell up and down, critically. He was, of course, tall; and was on the thin side. A smart young man, aged twenty-two, according to his papers, with an intelligent face and a firm mouth. The uniform was immaculate, the

13

boots shone with much diligent spit-and-polish, the brass of buttons and belt-buckle shone too. The belt's white pipeclay would have outshone a tablecloth in Buckingham Palace itself. Ogilvie cleared his throat preparatorily; in truth, he would have wished the interview to have taken place informally. This parade-ground stuff, he thought, was unfair to Campbell and unfair to him as well. To interview a man for entry into his regiment who wished to transfer out of his own was far from easy in front of the rejected regiment's senior personnel, but it couldn't be helped. This was the Guards; Lord Dornoch would have ordered it very differently.

Thus feeling at a disadvantage, Ogilvie stated the obvious. 'You wish to transfer to my regiment, Campbell.'

'Sir!'

'Why?'

Campbell's face began to flush; there was no flicker of expression on any of the other faces. Ogilvie waited. After a pause Campbell said, 'I wish for a commission, sir.'

There was a very faint stir from the Regimental Sergeant-Major, a motionless stir, a stir of feeling rather than movement, an emanation of something like seething im-

patience with guardsmen who had the impertinence to think themselves good enough
to join the officers as an equal. Ogilvie said,
'Yes, I see. Do you think you'll have a better
chance with us than with your own
regiment?'

'I hope so, sir.'

'I think you'd better explain that.'

'Sir! I think I am a poor guardsman, sir.'

Ogilvie smiled. 'That's honest at all events!
Tell me why you think that.'

'It's the ceremonial, sir.'

'We have that, too, you know.'

'Sir!'

Ogilvie didn't press; he understood, and
understood the better for his brief words
with MacTrease the night before. Campbell
didn't care for bull at every turn and Ogilvie
wasn't going to blame him for that, nor
would he force him to say so in his current
situation. He said, 'You realize, of course,
that my regiment's on Indian service.'

'Sir!'

'So you're prepared for that?'

'Sir!'

'We're stationed in Peshawar and are frequently in action against Pathan tribesmen
from Afghanistan.'

'I'd like to see–'

'Shut your mouth!' the Regimental Sergeant-Major bawled. 'Hold your tongue when you speak to officers! The officer didn't ask a question! The officer made a statement!'

Ogilvie gestured irritably with his hand. 'It's all right, Sar'nt-Major,' he said, recognizing the warrant officer as a bully and wishing he had his own RSM, Bosom Cunningham, at his side instead of an insensitive martinet. He turned back to Campbell. 'I gather you're prepared for active service?'

'Sir!'

'We still have some years to go in India. Do you consider yourself physically fit for a number of years in a largely unhealthy climate?'

'Sir!'

Ogilvie sighed inwardly; if only they said more than 'Sir!' in the Guards, life would be easier. He came now to what he was determined to say and never mind the assembled Guards faces. He said, 'If you transfer, Guardsman Campbell, you will transfer to something very different. You will transfer to a line regiment, a plain regiment of foot. Our standards are not a jot lower than yours, but they are different. We have less spit-and-polish, perhaps less glamour ... but

16

we spend rather more than half our service overseas and a good deal of that time in action that can be very unpleasant. We lose far more men than we would wish, and to be wounded in Afghanistan, say, is very nasty indeed for a variety of reasons – though we never leave our wounded behind if at all possible. Now, I gather from what you've said that you don't mind dropping the spit-and-polish, but I want to be very sure – since my Colonel will have your future career very much in mind – that you'll not miss the glamour and the London life. Well?'

Campbell took a deep breath, caught Ogilvie's eye for a moment, then looked aside at the RSM. He said, 'I want to be part of the real army, sir. I–'

'SHUT UP!' the Regimental Sergeant-Major roared, his face as scarlet as his tunic. The scandalized Adjutant nodded and Guardsman Campbell was about-turned and marched away. Ogilvie said mildly, 'I hadn't quite finished with Campbell, as a matter of fact. However, I'm impressed with him – I think he has courage–'

'Damned impertinence!'

'And I shall recommend my Colonel to accept him into my regiment, always assuming, of course, that your Colonel is willing to release him.'

'You may take the bloody man and good riddance,' the Adjutant said, and stalked rudely from the orderly room swishing his cane.

That night, Ogilvie travelled north by the train from King's Cross, bound for his family seat at Corriecraig Castle. With little more than a week to go before returning to India aboard the troopship from Portsmouth, he intended spending as long as possible visiting his father's tenants and crofters so that he could report to Sir Iain, who commanded the Northern Army in Murree, upon his return. During the long night journey Ogilvie's thoughts kept on returning to Guardsman Campbell, soon now to be Private Campbell of the 114th. Courage hadn't been a strong enough word when one considered the outraged faces and the quivering fury in the orderly room. On the other hand, it could have been desperation, the grasping of a lifeline; whatever it was, it had sounded like the honest truth. But a commission? On the assumption that Campbell was likely to get a poor report from his present colonel, an eventual commission didn't seem to be very firmly in prospect. The British Army didn't chuck commissions around the ranks, far from it. A man had to be outstanding, and he had to have served for five years during which time he had to have attained the rank of corporal or sergeant in theory, whilst in practice the rank of sergeant was usually necessary. Ogilvie reflected on the possibilities of the report from the Colonel of the Coldstream Guards; prior to the interview, he had spoken to the Adjutant and Company Commander and had been told that Campbell was a good soldier but appeared to lack the qualities of leadership that even a lance-corporal must have; there was a diffidence about him that did not inspire confidence. Well, time would tell. Campbell's background was perfectly suitable to sustain a commission; his father was a procurator fiscal in Inverness-shire, and was related, albeit distantly, to the Marquis of Breadalbane. There was enough money in the family to provide the private means so essential to an officer. Campbell had made up his mind late that he wished a military career; he had been side-tracked by his father into legal studies and by the time he had made his point that the law was not for him, he had missed his chance of Sandhurst or a commission via a university.

Keen he had to be: it must, Ogilvie thought, take a monumental keenness to induce any man of Campbell's station in life to undergo five years' hardship in the barrack-rooms and on the parade-grounds under the lashing tongues of the drill-sergeants of the Guards, men who on the whole did not take kindly to men whose ambitions if fulfilled would carry them above their heads.

Ogilvie reached Corriecraig soon after luncheon next day. All the way in the train north from Edinburgh he had looked out pleasurably at Scotland; this was not his first visit home since the regiment had embarked for India – he had had long leave some three years before – but Scotland called strongly across the seas and Ogilvie could scarcely wait to be met by the station-wagon at Aviemore and then to see the faces of his father's servants, faces familiar since early childhood, faces that were as much a part of the family as were those of his parents and sister.

This time, however, he was not to be left long in disregard of regimental matters. He had scarcely had time to go up to his room when a boy on a bicycle brought a telegram from the depot, across the Monadliath Mountains at Invermore, instructing him to report as soon as possible.

Two

In the depot, there were few familiar faces; only the depot Sergeant-Major and the officer in charge, a Major Leish, whom Ogilvie remembered as a captain when he had first gone out to India. Leish had received a cable from Peshawar – from Lord Dornoch.

'Trouble,' Leish said briefly. 'Your brigade's been ordered out. Some rajah or other has rebelled against the Raj.'

Ogilvie asked, 'Which Rajah?'

'Drosh. I've looked up the maps. Drosh is on the–'

'Chitral River.'

Leish looked up. 'You know the place?'

Ogilvie gave a humourless laugh. 'I know it all right, Major. I know the Rajah of Drosh, too. I wish I didn't.'

'Oh. Like that, is it?'

21

Ogilvie got to his feet and moved across to the window of the Major's office. He looked out at the mountains, green and purple, stark against a pale sky as the sun went down. Soon there would be splendid sunset colours in that sky; it wasn't so different from the mountain ranges of the North-West Frontier, except that Scotland didn't hold anyone quite like the scheming Rajah of Drosh. Ogilvie brought out a silver cigarette-case and thoughtfully tapped a cigarette on it before offering the case to the Major.

Taking one, Leish said remindingly, 'The Rajah of Drosh, Ogilvie.'

'Yes.' Ogilvie lit his cigarette, inhaling deeply. He said, 'Rajah Mohan Singh is a bastard.'

'Literally?'

Ogilvie grinned. 'That depends on what you mean by bastard in India! All those wives ... anyway, he's a bastard by nature. Fabulously rich, of course – rooms full of diamonds and rubies, the usual sort of thing. He rules by fear, not that that of itself is remarkable since they all do more or less. But Drosh is said to have dungeons full of his enemies or those who have displeased him in some way. He maintains torture chambers too, so it's said. He's a filthy little man in every way, food all down his clothing, smells like a sewer and looks like a rat. His loyalties have always been suspect, but so far he's kept his nose clean – because he has to. Drosh is not so far off Afghanistan, and he's a Hindu isolated among a hell of a lot of Muslims.'

'And the Raj keeps him safe?'

Ogilvie nodded. 'That's why I'm surprised. Have you any details?'

'Of the overall scene, politically, no. Dornoch's cable simply said that the battalion had had a lot of casualties – no names, but it seems he's lost a hundred and ten NCOs and men. That's big.'

'My God!' Ogilvie stared in concern. 'I only hope Bosom Cunningham's all right–'

'I assume he is. NCOs and men ... no mention of a warrant officer. However, the point of your visit here is this: Dornoch's cable was by way of a warning that Northern Command will be asking for a draft from the depot, a draft to be embarked with you aboard the *Jumna* for Bombay. The Colonel asked for you and Colour MacTrease to put 'em through their paces before they leave, seeing that they'll be going straight into action on arrival.' Leish paused and then remarked somewhat sadly, 'We're out of touch here at Invermore, you see. It's a backwater, and Indian fighting's largely a closed book as far as we're concerned.'

'Like the Coldstream,' Ogilvie said, then added, 'I don't really mean that about a fine regiment, but–'

'Guardsman Campbell?'

'Yes. You've heard about him, Major?'

Leish nodded. 'I've had a telegram. He's joining the depot in two days' time.'

'I'm glad to hear it. I suggest he joins the India draft.'

Leish said doubtfully, 'Early days, don't you think?'

'Perhaps, but–'

'I'd thought of holding him until the next replacements are asked for, give him a chance to learn our ways, that sort of thing.'

Ogilvie hummed a tune between his teeth. After a moment he said, 'The decision's yours, of course, Major. But how about watching him, see how he develops in the few days available? After all, he's had two years' Guards training. It can't all have been wasted.'

Leish said, 'All right, I'll go along with that. He's one of these gentlemen rankers, I understand ... and as you say, two years in already.'

'Yes. We don't want to hold up his prospects. He's got three years to do ... if he goes beyond that he'll be too far behind in the promotion stakes. He's twenty-two already.'

Word was sent to Corriecraig for Ogilvie's kit to be brought over; and he slept that night in a small room in the depot. By the time he was up next morning, volunteers for India had already been called for and the list had been heavily over-subscribed: foreign service was what a man joined the army for in most cases, though poverty and the lack of employment were often enough the initial prod. Ogilvie had the volunteers fallen in after a quick breakfast, and spoke to them on parade, giving them the brief facts so far as he knew them of the battalion's current engagement on the North-West Frontier and telling them something of what to expect on Indian service, especially when attached to Northern Command, which was where the fighting tended to be and where, when out on distant patrol, the killing shots from the *jezails* carried by the Pathans came without warning. He spoke to them of the use of the knife, and of *thuggee*. He warned them that the ways of campaigning in India were very different from manoeuvres at

25

home, but added that, as Scots, they would at least be well used to the mountain terrain in which their fighting would lie.

'We have five days,' he said. 'Five days, before we entrain for Portsmouth. Make the most of it. Colour-Sergeant MacTrease and I intend to drive you hard. Listen to what we say, and it just may save your life when you get to India.'

Later that day MacTrease arrived from Glasgow, not sorry to be removed with a perfect excuse from his sister's home; Mac-Trease was a soldier to his finger-tips, happy only when with the regiment and when able to take a dram without being looked at askance. His voice was soon heard, loudly raised over the parade-ground as he drilled and instructed his replacement draft, which was just over full company strength. The following day ex-Guardsman Campbell arrived from London, in *mufti*, and was taken in hand by MacTrease, who sent him to the quartermaster's store for kitting-out as a private in a Highland regiment.

'You can forget the bloody boots,' Ogilvie heard MacTrease say.

Campbell was momentarily disconcerted. 'No boots, Colour-Sar'nt?'

'Wheesht, man, o' course there are boots!

What I meant was, in the 114th we don't *carry* the Jocks onto parade like the Guards, so their boots don't get dusty before inspection. You'll be finding all the dust in the world when you reach India ... mind, we don't expect the boots to be dirty, but there are limits – right?'

'Right, Colour-Sar'nt.'

'Awa' wi' ye, then.'

Campbell, who had remained stiffly at attention throughout, turned about smartly and with a crash of the offending boots or their civilian equivalents. He marched away; no recruit-like shuffling. His bearing seemed to please MacTrease, who had a word with Ogilvie soon after.

'He's no' bad, Captain Ogilvie, sir, but I'll not pre-judge. We can take his drill for granted, o' course, but the Lord knows what he'll look like in the kilt.'

Ogilvie smiled. 'Damn it all, Colour, he's a Scot!'

'Aye. A trewed one, maybe. Not all the Scots wear the kilt, sir, and he has long, skinny legs. The best wearers o' the kilt, sir, have a *firm* look rather than a spindly one.'

'Like you?' Ogilvie suggested with a straight face.

'If you say so, sir.'

'I do,' Ogilvie responded with a grin. 'So stop blowing your own sartorial trumpet, Colour, and prepare the draft to fall-in in half an hour, in full marching order. I want to try to simulate a patrol under Frontier conditions, and Campbell will come with us, though he's not yet positively detailed for India.' He opened his map case and brought out a map of the Monadliath Mountains. He traced a route with his finger. 'We'll march out along there – you see? I've arranged with the Major for the rest of the holding battalion to scatter in the hills and act as Pathans, and we'll just see what happens.'

Throughout the day the Scots were kept hard at it, marching through the glens and along the high passes that were so like the Afghan border on a smaller scale. MacTrease was constantly shaking his head and clicking his tongue and bawling at men who in India would have been dead ten times over. Ogilvie kept his eye on Private Campbell whenever he could. The man seemed conscientious rather than leaderlike, though it was perhaps not fair to him to make that assessment: no opportunity for leadership in fact cropped up, and no sensible man would stick his neck out too far in the first few days with a new regiment, the more so as he came from the Guards. And at least Campbell conducted himself as a soldier, obeying orders instantly and with precision. Ogilvie was reasonably impressed, and remained so during the succeeding days of exercise; and as the time for entraining drew near was able to recommend to Leish that Campbell should be detailed for India with the others. The Major, who had also watched the re-placement draft from time to time, agreed. As a basic soldier, Campbell was in fact more experienced than those among the Scots who had only recently moved out of the recruits' squad.

Only MacTrease seemed displeased.

He said, 'The man's a plank of wood, sir. His reactions are automatic.'

'As a soldier's should be, Colour.'

'Up to a point, sir, yes. That's what the Coldstream will have taught him for sure, so maybe he has to unlearn. The thing is, sir, as you know yourself, in action in India a man has to think for himself, and quickly, too, often enough. When acting as a picquet, for example, a man hasn't a colour-sergeant behind him every minute of his duty.'

'True. But woodenness isn't unusual. We have our share of wooden men already!'

'Then we don't need more, sir, when we have the chance to pick and choose in his case. Besides, he aspires to be an officer, no less!' MacTrease sucked his teeth. 'Wooden officers can kill good men, sir.'

Ogilvie said crisply, 'That's a different consideration, Colour. For now and the forseeable future, he's a private with the makings of a good one in my opinion, and I shall be glad to have him in the draft.'

'As you say, sir.'

The following day the draft was marched to the railway station to entrain for Portsmouth where they would be joined by B Company under Ogilvie's subalterns. They marched behind the pipes and drums to the cheers of the local populace who had turned out to a man to wave Godspeed to soldiers about to embark for India, men who would not return to Invermore for many a long year if at all. There was always sadness in a departure for foreign service; too many of the marching men were sons or brothers, husbands in a few cases where men had taken the dire plunge of marrying "off the strength" and could not take their wives with them. So tears were mingled with the cheering and the handkerchiefs were out for more than waving. As the train pulled out

the strains of Auld Lang Syne came haunt-
ingly from the pipes and the lumps came to
many throats. Ogilvie, looking from the
window as the steam wreathed overhead,
found himself thinking of his own first
departure from Invermore with the whole
battalion, and the pipers playing the tune
composed specially for their leaving by Pipe-
Major-Ross – Farewell to Invermore. That
tune had been heard many times since in the
years between, heard sounding clear over
the Afghan hills or the Indian plain or the
great mountains of Kashmir, bringing with
it its heartfelt memories of Scotland, bringing, as the pipes always did, the feeling of
Scotland all the way to distant shores and
distant battles in the name of Empire.

India.

Some three weeks later they were there,
and disembarking at Princes Dock in the
great teeming city of Bombay, while the
Jumna waited to embark the time-expired
men and steam them home to England and
their families. Many nostalgic looks were
cast back at the troopship, last link with
home, as the draft together with many other
units for the reinforcement of Northern
Command marched out for the railway

station and the many smells and sounds of the sub-continent. Three days later they de-trained at Peshawar, not so far from the Khyber Pass, and were marched the two miles westwards into the Royal Strathspey's cantonment. Ogilvie was expecting to be on the march again before nightfall, moving north to join the rest of the battalion towards Drosh; and was surprised to find the Scots in cantonments after all. Bosom Cunningham, Regimental Sergeant-Major, square and solid, was at the gate as B Company and the new draft marched in; he ran a critical eye over the latter in particular, and slammed to the salute as Ogilvie passed; and Ogilvie detached for a word with him as the men were marched across the square by MacTrease.

'Welcome back, sir,' Cunningham said.

'Thank you, Sarn't-Major.' Ogilvie touch-ed the ribbon of the Military Medal that had joined the others on Cunningham's tunic. That had been recommended during the last action in which Ogilvie had taken part before going to London, and the ribbon was very new. 'Congratulations. It was well earned.'

'Thank you, sir.'

Ogilvie said, 'Well, it's good to be back

32

with the regiment ... but I'm told you've had a rough time of it.'

'Aye, sir, we have and that's a fact. It was murder, up by Drosh. The buggers came down upon us at the ford across the Chitral, and caught us in enfilading fire. We've lost some good men, Captain Ogilvie.'

'And the regiment's back. Why's that?'

'Not the Colonel's wish, sir. Orders came by the field telegraph to withdraw.'

'And the reason?'

Cunningham looked away across Ogilvie's shoulder. 'I do not know the reason, sir. Tell me, Captain Ogilvie, if you will: how were things at Invermore?'

'Much as usual, Sar'nt-Major. It doesn't change, nor do the Jocks. Practically all the holding battalion volunteered as replacements. I think I've brought you a good bunch.'

'Well, if they're not good now, sir, they soon will be, I guarantee. I think you're wanted, sir.' Cunningham gestured, and Ogilvie turned to find the Adjutant's runner hovering. The man saluted, presented Captain Black's compliments and would Captain Ogilvie attend the battalion office immediately. The Regimental Sergeant-Major turned away and Ogilvie strode across the parade-ground, wondering about Cunningham's obvious reluctance to discuss the reason for the recent withdrawal from the vicinity of Drosh. There was something odd in the air; Cunningham didn't normally dissemble, but Ogilvie felt pretty sure the RSM had known the reason for that withdrawal.

Lord Dornoch was with Andrew Black when Ogilvie reported to the battalion office. He welcomed Ogilvie warmly while the Adjutant stood dour and gloomy as ever, pulling at a moustache as black as his name. Black was not a smiling man. Pleasantries over, the Colonel took Ogilvie's formal report of the Royal Strathspey's part in the Queen's celebrations and of the newly arrived replacements from Invermore; then he gave an account of the action against Rajah Mohan Singh and an exposition of the background to the Rajah's rebellion. Mohan Singh, he said, had never been particular about his temporary allies – Hindu or Muslim, they were all the same to him in the pursuit of wealth and power – and this time he was thought to have allied himself to Afghanistan – to the Amir in Kabul. 'It's a shaky enough alliance,' Dornoch said, 'and both sides must know it, but Mohan Singh may well believe it'll last his purpose, and his purpose happens to be a particularly nasty one. In brief, the little so-and-so's providing a safe route for the smuggling of young women across the Frontier – some going out for Persia and other places, some being diverted into His Highness' harem, no doubt – and others coming the other way for delivery to the wife markets in Madras and elsewhere. They're not pretty places.'

They were not; Ogilvie had seen the wife markets, where women changed hands for cash or goods, some of them even sold by their own husbands. They had been a mixed bunch, some ugly, some good-looking, some young and some not so young, going cheap. It could not be denied that many of them had accepted their lot philosophically or that some had been brazen about it, glad to be found by a man as it were at any price. But the majority had had a hopeless look about them, a wan look, and many had been crying as they were inspected by the customers or led away by a new master; and many had been girls from beyond the frontiers of India, a real mix of races, Burmese, Chinese, Malayan, Persian. As a trade it was diabolical, but His Highness of Drosh, adding much to his riches by way of it, would have no scruples at all.

'There's worse,' Lord Dornoch said abruptly. There was a sound of disgust in his voice and he moved his shoulders as though wishing that something could be shrugged off and never spoken of. At his side, Black rolled his eyes heavenwards with more than a touch of unction. Then Dornoch dropped his bombshell. He said in a voice filled with strain, 'There's something you'll have to know, James. All the officers are aware of it, so is Cunningham, but one can only hope it's gone no further. The Major's missing ... he had leave to Simla and he failed to return – this much, of course, all ranks know about. I'm not in the habit of lying to the men, thus I have never sanctioned a fabrication through the grapevine – for instance that the Major was given extended leave. Enquiries were made and nothing was known of Lord Brora in Simla other than that he had been there and had left presumably to rejoin the regiment. Naturally, the facts were reported to Brigade and then to Division, and when we marched out for Drosh cavalry patrols were ordered out from all garrisons south-east of Peshawar to search the country between here and Simla, in case the Major had been ambushed and taken by bandits. But there was no spoor, no evidence at all to support the theory of an ambush.' Dornoch paused. 'We now come to the reason we were ordered to withdraw. A report came from Division by means of a mounted runner – a report to say Lord Brora was known to be in Drosh.'

'In Drosh?' Ogilvie repeated wonderingly.

'In the palace with His Highness.'

'What for, Colonel?'

Dornoch lifted his hands in the air, palms uppermost. 'The whole thing is very disturbing. It seems a communication had been delivered to General Fettleworth in Nowshera, to the effect that Lord Brora had pledged the name of the Raj, promising that His Highness would not be attacked or in any way inconvenienced over this matter of the women, which was not the concern of British India but a matter for the native states alone. Since Drosh owes allegiance to the Raj, that's obvious balderdash. But the brigade was withdrawn pending consultations with Calcutta and word is still awaited from there. What Lord Brora is up to I know not, nor how he came to be in Drosh. It could be kidnap and then force applied to get his signature to a document – I don't know and neither does anyone else at this stage. There could have been a lure ... the Major is something of an enigma, as we all know, and he is a womanizer – I shall say no more about that. But the fact remains that he is highly connected and his word carries weight, which His Highness will be well aware of. It seems that Calcutta is reluctant to disown Brora's word until a good deal more is known.'

Black put in a word at that point. He said, 'In the meantime, the trade in women will doubtless be continuing.'

Before luncheon, the talk in the ante-room was all of Brora, at least until the Colonel entered when the gossip and speculation stopped. The Major was far from being a popular man in the mess, and was detested by the rank and file for his loud, arrogant manner and his bullying; there was an inclination to assume the worst – that Brora had become a renegade, throwing in his lot with the Rajah of Drosh for what he could get out of in the way of women and money. Despite his position as a belted earl, Brora was known not to be a rich man. It was rumoured that his estates in Scotland were mortgaged to the hilt. He could have seen a way out. Against this was his known antipathy towards natives; he loathed them and lost no opportunity of saying so, loudly, in their hearing. He would make a strange confederate for His Highness of Drosh unless he could control his temper, which was unlikely. Thieves, if that was what this was all about, might soon fall out and certainly neither the Rajah nor Brora were strong on honour. Brora, though a first-class officer in the field, had no scruples when it came to his own interests, regimentally or otherwise. Ogilvie still smarted now and again over Brora's attempts to have both him and Cunningham Court Martialled on trumped up charges. Yet Ogilvie found it hard to equate any officer with the sort of crime that was being suggested in whispers around the ante-room; at some time or other an explanation would come. In the meantime the battalion seemed to be in a kind of suspension, waiting for the next move. No-one doubted that they would be ordered out again soon with their brigaded battalions. Luncheon was a gloomy affair what with one thing and another; no-one liked the retreat that had taken place and no-one liked the casualties. Many familiar faces had gone from the parade when the men fell in, among them too many seasoned and reliable sergeants and corporals who would be hard to replace. Promotions had had to be made from the best men available, but it would be a while yet before the new NCOs had settled down to their responsibilities. With promotions in mind, Ogilvie approached the Adjutant after the meal was finished, before Black retired to his quarter for his afternoon nap.

He said, 'You'll be aware I brought a gentleman ranker out from home, Andrew.'

'Yes. What's he like?'

'Rather soon to say, but I think he'll prove a good soldier.'

'Good enough for a commission, which I understand from the Colonel he's after?'

'I don't know. I think we have to find that out as soon as possible, in fairness to Campbell himself. Time is passing. There's only one way to find out, Andrew: he'll have to be watched for a while, then made up to lance.'

'If he's worth it.'

'He has to have his chance to show what he can do when he's in a position of responsibility.' Ogilvie paused. 'Currently, there are vacancies for lance-corporals, aren't there?'

Black nodded. 'Yes, indeed there are. But I take it you're not suggesting he be made lance now, are you?'

'No. I–'

'I'm glad,' Black said tartly. 'You shouldn't need to be told it's far too soon–'

'He's had two years in the Guards already, Andrew.'

Black clicked his tongue. 'Yes, yes. I know that. But that's part of the difficulty. We can't give him preference on account of the Guards – there'd be all manner of friction and bad feeling in the battalion and frankly I wouldn't blame the men at all.'

Ogilvie said, 'I'm really only suggesting that we watch Campbell with a view to a stripe – that's all. I agree with what you say about bad feeling–'

'Which would come largely because he *didn't* get his stripe from the Coldstream, James. What was not good enough for the Guards is good enough for Scots. Do you follow me?'

Ogilvie blew out a long breath; the Adjutant was right enough, but it was hard luck if Campbell was in effect to have the Guards held against him. On the other hand, a keen and efficient soldier with his sights set on the officers' mess should have made lance within two years, as MacTrease had remarked back in Chelsea barracks. Time would tell and Ogilvie hoped it would tell in Campbell's favour. The atmosphere in that orderly room in Wellington Barracks had pre-disposed him towards Campbell and whilst aboard the troopship he had had a couple of unofficial talks with the man and had come to like him. He was about to say more to Black when a visitor entered the ante-room: Major Blaise-Willoughby, the Political Officer from Division, as scruffy as ever in a crumpled white suit showing traces of gravy, and with his pet monkey, Wolseley, chattering away from his left shoulder.

'Ah, Ogilvie,' Blaise-Willoughby said. 'I was told you were back after adding your lustre to Her Majesty's jubilee procession ... and you come back to sad tidings. I'm sorry.'

'Can we do anything for you, Blaise-Willoughby?' Black asked, looking pointedly at the clock: the time for siesta was passing.

'Not until I've had words with your Colonel, Black. Just one thing, though ... is it too late for a *chota peg* by any chance? I don't like to bum, but–'

Looking sour, Black called for a bearer. 'A *chota peg* for Major Blaise-Willoughby – on the mess account, not mine.'

Blaise-Willoughby said, 'Very decent of the mess, and I thank all concerned.' He sat

42

down and closed his eyes, looking thoroughly shop-soiled and worn, until the whisky
came. He took it in two mouthfuls, with
little soda in it, then said, 'I'll be off to see
Lord Dornoch, then.'

'He'll not be pleased,' Black said.

'No, I don't believe he will.' Blaise-Willoughby paused. 'There's been word of your
Major, and it's not nice.'

Saying nothing further, he left the ante-
room.

Three

Indian afternoon or not, the Colonel, after a
brief talk with Blaise-Willoughby, sent for all
the officers to come to his bungalow, the
Regimental Sergeant-Major included. He
wasted no time; his face bleak, his mouth
twitching a little at the corners, he said, 'I
have a report from Major Blaise-Willoughby, gentlemen. I think you should all hear it
and thereafter keep it to yourselves and do
your best to stifle any grapevines operating
in the barrack-rooms – and in the Sergeants'

43

Mess, Mr Cunningham.'

'I'll do that, sir.'

'Thank you. I'll not keep you long.' Dornoch cleared his throat. 'Major Blaise-Willoughby has made contact with a Hindu trader from Peshawar, a man who knows Lord Brora well – he's a dealer in leather-work, and has made harness for Brora's sister-in-law's horse and that of his niece when they were staying here. This man was in the town of Garwar when he saw Brora entering the house of another Hindu known to be involved in the trade with women. Possibly with blackmail in mind in the first instance, he hid himself and watched through a window. He saw Brora in conversation with the woman-trader, and he saw a bag of what he believed to be money passed over. The two appeared to be very friendly, and after some half an hour they both rode out of Garwar – separately, but each was heading in the general direction of the Chitral River, and, possibly, Drosh.' Dornoch was standing very stiffly, very straight, with his shoulders drawn back. 'In the end, the trader put his loyalty to the Raj above black-mail, and reported fully to Major Blaise-Willoughby. This report has been forwarded to Northern Army in Murree. That is all,

44

Blaise-Willoughby scowled. 'By God, he would have been if I'd had anything to do with it! My job's hard enough without bloody stupid amateurs queering the pitch. I can do without that sort of thing, thank you very much.'

Ogilvie lifted an eyebrow. 'I don't count as an amateur, then?'

'Don't be bloody wet. If you were, I wouldn't touch you with a barge pole.' Blaise-Willoughby studied him through narrowed eyes as the filthy native clothing went on. 'As a matter of fact you're getting almost as professional as me. Ever thought of transferring, Ogilvie?'

'To the Political?' Ogilvie sounded incredulous. 'Rather not! I'm quite happy with my regiment, Major.'

Blaise-Willoughby sniffed. 'It's a wasted talent,' he said. Ogilvie made no response; basically, he and Blaise-Willoughby were poles apart. He had no desire to live a life of intrigue and deviousness; Blaise-Willoughby seemed to thrive on it. While Ogilvie finished his transformation into a native itinerant trader, the Political Officer called for a runner to make arrangements for the care of Wolseley during his absence.

It was Colour-Sergeant MacTrease who

47

came to Wolseley's assistance; he knew the monkey of old and felt some compassion for its nomadic existence, shoulder-borne from here to there and back again, often enough with its master mounted. MacTrease went into B Company's barrack-room, where the men were polishing buttons and badges and giving their rifles a pull-through with strips of two-by-four.

'Private Campbell!' he shouted.

From the far end of the barrack-room a minor explosion seemed to take place. Boots slammed into the floor as a body came upright to attention and then marched stiffly, with arms swinging from the shoulder, the length of the room. Campbell halted with another slam of boots, one-one-two.

'Colour-Sar'nt!'

MacTrease nodded, concealing a grin. 'Very smart, very smart indeed.' There were titters from the rest of the men. 'Now, Private Campbell, you're a gentleman it's said. I'll not call upon you to confirm that or to deny it. I have a special job for you, right?'

'Colour-Sar'nt!' The eyes stared over Mac-Trease's head.

'Gentlemen are addicted to pets. Dogs and such. They are good with them. Also horses. Am I not right?'

'Colour-Sar'nt!'

MacTrease let out a long breath. 'By the Lord God Almighty,' he said in a loud voice, 'you're no longer in the Coldstream so you may speak as a human being, Private Campbell. When making the affirmative, you are permitted to say *yes* in the 114th. Do you understand me?'

Campbell swallowed then said, 'Yes, Colour-Sar'nt.'

'Good! That's much better. Now, as to your duties. Do you know what they are to be?'

'To look after an officer's dogs or horses, Colour-Sar'nt.'

MacTrease grinned. 'Not quite. You will proceed at once to the orderly room, Private Campbell, where you will take delivery of one monkey name of Wolseley, so called after His Lordship the Commander-in-Chief at the Horse Guards, the property of the Divisional Political Officer. And God help you if you let the little bugger escape.'

Authenticity was the keynote, always, when attempting to penetrate a native environment in native dress. As ever, Blaise-Willoughby left nothing to chance: every British cantonment had its quota of natives – bear-

49

ers, *syces* for the horses, *nappis* amd *chikkos* for the morning shaving of the troops in their beds, *chaukidahs* to patrol the compounds and keep intruders away, *khansammas* for the cooking, *bhistis* to bring the bath water ... *punkah-wallahs, ayahs, malis* and their boy assistants to keep the compounds clean and tidy. Most of these would be loyal to their sahibs and mem'sahibs and to the Raj – many of them loyal to the death – but a few would not be, the few who might have been disaffected by the unruly elements in the bazaars, the speech-makers and the soft speakers who plotted to remove the British from the subcontinent. From these few, news could fly with astonishing swiftness if strange natives were seen to hobnob with the garrison and then to walk freely from the barrack gate. So Blaise-Willoughby, with Ogilvie, put on a small melodrama. The two officers sneaked out from a window and then slunk along the verandah outside it, eyes darting, bodies flattened to the wall. At a pre-arranged signal a drill-sergeant gave a warning shout, and the guard was turned out at the double. Blaise-Willoughby and Ogilvie took to their heels, making swiftly, as also pre-arranged, for the back regions of the cantonment. As they neared the perimeter fence, running hell for leather, the barrack guard opened fire with live ammunition. Their aim being naturally poor, bullets snicked off fences and buildings, humming around the two supposed marauders as they flung themselves at the high fence and scaled it. From the top, Ogilvie jumped down to the other side. Bullets sped over and there was a realistic howl of pain from Blaise-Willoughby, who dropped like a stone, landing in a heap on the ground.

'Are you all right?' Ogilvie asked.

'No!'

'Broken anything?'

'No!' The Political Officer sat up, then pulled himself to his feet as the firing continued. There was a tear in the back of his native garment and a trickle of blood ran down his bare right leg. 'Clumsy buggers ... snicked my arse. They had no need to be that realistic, Ogilvie. I'd be obliged if you'd damn well tell them so. I wouldn't be surprised if it was done quite intentionally – the bloody infantry's childish enough for that, and you damn soldiers never seem to appreciate what the Political does for you–' Blaise-Willoughby broke off, glaring angrily. 'What the hell are you grinning for, Ogilvie?'

★ ★ ★

In Nowshera, some thirty miles east of the Peshawar cantonment, Lieutenant-General Francis Fettleworth – Bloody Francis to his soldiers – Commander of the First Division of Northern Army and in his own view a man to be reckoned with, was staring in much concern at a case of Dewar's whisky lying smashed outside his quarters and surrounded by a group of chattering natives. Fettleworth's eyes bulged and his white walrus moustache seemed to quiver: whisky was essential to life in India and it so happened that Northern Army was going through a shortage, which was all the fault of the blasted Supply and Transport, whose colonel was going to be made to suffer for his corps' deficiencies.

'Who did this?' Fettleworth demanded. 'Damn waste! Damn disgrace!'

The Chief of Staff shrugged wearily; he had had a full day of Bloody Francis already, and had now been bidden to dine with his General. 'It's not the end of the world, sir. One case of whisky, two pounds ten shillings sterling—'

'It's not that, Lakenham, it's the damn shortage. You'll have to draw me more stocks from the HQ mess and some of the damn staff officers can go without – they

52

drink too much in any case, it's a scandal. I ask again: *who did it?*'

'I really don't know, sir–'

'Find out, then. A bloody lakh of rupees to sixpence it's my bloody Number One bearer, the old fool's senile. I'll have his arse kicked for him, damned if I won't.' Bloody Francis shook both hands in the air, cane and all; his khaki-drill tunic rose above his ample stomach while crossed swords and stars rose and fell upon his shoulders, twinkling in the light from a guard lantern as dusk fell over India. 'As though I haven't enough to contend with, what with this blasted Drosh business and that oaf Brora!'

'I'd not use that expression at the moment, sir.'

'Oh, wouldn't you?' Fettleworth stared belligerently. 'Well, I would and do. Oaf I said, and oaf I meant. It has nothing to do with his guilt or otherwise, though I'd take my wager the bloody man *is* guilty. Get rid of these blasted natives, Lakenham. I'll have them questioned later. In the meantime I'm hungry.' He rubbed his hands together as Lakenham nodded at the ADC, who dispersed the natives with shouts and threatening gestures. Bloody Francis Fettleworth was ever a hearty trencherman; even when upon the march in hostile territory, he insisted upon a full menu, properly served with clean napery and silver set out upon his trestle table. Followed by his Chief of Staff and ADC, he entered his residence to find his wife waiting and looking immensely anxious.

'Well, m'dear,' Bloody Francis said huffily, giving the dried-up cheek, yellowish from long years beneath the Indian sun, a peck. 'You'll have heard about my whisky I dare say. I hope all's well with the commissariat, hey?'

'Yes, Francis–'

'Well, thank God for that–'

'But there isn't any whisky, dear.'

'No whisky?' Fettleworth's face grew mottled. 'Did you say *no* whisky? No whisky at all?'

'No, dear. I'm dreadfully sorry.' Hands were wrung and the General's lady trembled, her face now more ashen than yellow. 'There's sherry–'

'Sherry! Sherry my backside, sherry's a bloody woman's tipple! I won't have sherry, d'you hear! Lakenham?'

'I'd much appreciate a glass, sir,' Brigadier-General Lakenham said.

Fettleworth made a hissing noise. 'I wasn't

asking you to have a sherry, blast you, I was suggesting you stir yourself and send for a bottle of Dewar's from the bloody mess.'

The ADC stepped forward. 'I'll go at once, sir.'

The HQ mess was not far away; conversation languished during the ADC's absence, as though at this time of the evening the Divisional Commander could be fuelled only by Dewar's. His lady wife did her best and engaged Brigadier-General Lakenham in a discourse upon the ballet, a subject in which the Chief of Staff was not well versed, which became all too plain; and the conversation veered towards a monologue on polo and pig-sticking, subjects somewhat foreign to Mrs Fettleworth. When the whisky arrived, by which time Fettleworth had gone off to change into a dinner jacket, so did dinner; and during the course of it Fettleworth, thanks to Dewar's, mellowed enough to mutter a complimentary remark about the curry.

'Damn good. Probably horse, but it's hot. Now, this feller, Lakenham, this blasted native – Drosh.'

'Yes, sir?'

'He can't be left to – to.' Fettleworth broke off in some embarrassment. It was not done to mention prostitution and harems and wife markets in front of wives who should know nothing of such things. Wives, after all, were white. But there was a pressing need to discuss the Rajah of Drosh, notwithstanding that he had been discussing him for many days now, because an idea, a good one, had just smitten home. Ideas fled fast if you didn't pursue them immediately. So Fettleworth chased his bearers out of earshot, cleared his throat and glared the length of the dinner table towards his wife. When she didn't respond he cleared and glared again, then, when he had caught her eye, he jerked his head towards the bead curtain across the doorway, outside which the *punkah-wallah* sat with legs outstretched on the floor interminably pulling a cord to give a stir of air to the sahibs in the dining-room.

'M'dear,' Fettleworth said, jerking again, twice. He was beginning to sound cross, and Mrs Fettleworth became agitated in response.

'The pudding, Francis. We've not yet–'

'Oh, bugger the pudding, too much sog isn't good for you in any case–'

'Francis!'

'I'm asking you to pretend you've had it. I'm asking you to simulate the port stage.

Oh my God!' Fettleworth thumped a fist on the table and things danced. 'Don't you understand, for heaven's sake?'

'But–'

'Don't argue, m'dear, don't argue. Just go.'

Close to tears, the General's lady got up and left the room, walking fast. Lakenham, who, like the youthful ADC, had kept his eyes on his plate throughout the exchange, wondered how she put up with it, indeed how anybody at Division put up with their bombastic commander. Fettleworth released the button of his dinner jacket and allowed his stomach to expand: it looked as though it had had an excess of pudding in its time. He gave a sigh of relief.

'The mem'sahib's all very well,' he said. 'I'm fond of her, goes without saying – but there are limits. She's had a sheltered up-bringing – her father was the Dean of Truro. Now we can talk, and I believe I've found the answer to that dirty little rajah feller.'

Lakenham cocked an eye at his lord and master and looked more or less expectant, but not particularly hopeful. Most of Bloody Francis' ideas were non-starters. Fettleworth went on, 'That young Ogilvie of the 114th. Sir Iain's boy.'

Lakenham sipped whisky; a small one, a

mere *burra peg* since the availability was limited to the one bottle. He asked, 'What about him?'

'Blaise-Willoughby's taken him off on some mission in Garwar – the wife market.' Fettleworth gave a coarse chuckle. 'They'll see some sights, damned if they won't! There's a lot of ordinary prostitution in Garwar too – so I've been told. They expose themselves at the windows, you know.'

'Really.'

'Oh, yes. Breasts ... even other things. A filthy business, of course, one that I can't approve, but they do serve their purpose and rid the troops of a good deal of dirty water as the saying goes.'

'And give them something else in exchange,' Lakenham said. 'The medical men are always complaining about it–'

'Damn leeches complain about everything, like farmers. But Ogilvie now: depending on what Blaise-Willoughby's report is, depending, don't you know, on what the two of them unearth, I've half a mind to send young Ogilvie in as an *agent provocateur*.'

'Send him in where?'

'Drosh. The palace! See what he can dig up. Find Brora perhaps. If he can be seen amongst the fleas and lice – I've been in the place and it's filthy, quite insanitary and women everywhere. You can't pee without splashing one of them. I went to a – a levee I suppose you'd call it, once. That was when poor Fowler had your job – you'll remember the story, of course.'

Lakenham nodded. Poor Fowler – Brigadier-General Fowler – had come to grief and Cheltenham during that levee in Drosh, having been discovered by a highly-placed Civilian from the India Office when upon a pile of cushions with one of the Rajah's concubines; poor Fowler had been summarily retired after the Civilian, a prim man, had sent in his colourful report. Division had heard later that the concubine had been buried in the earth with only her head showing above, and then a harrow had been run over her and had decapitated her. Lakenham, who was a broad-minded man, hoped that the Civilian had been able to live with his conscience thereafter. He asked, 'What would Ogilvie be expected to do, sir?'

'What I said – dig things up, then return–'

'Easier said than done, I fear.'

'Well, I *don't* fear,' Bloody Francis said nastily. 'The Raj wasn't won by namby-pambyism as I dare say I've said before now.

I've no time for cowards in my Division. Ogilvie will dig things up, then return and report. Upon his report, I shall base my submissions to Murree. Sir Iain's bound to trust his own boy, stands to reason, and he'll act on my report. The thing is, don't you see, until I know where I stand I can't move.'

'Quite, sir,' Lakenham said with a tinge of sarcasm. 'Shall I take it you wish Dornoch to have Ogilvie sent up to Division when he gets back from Garwar?'

'Yes,' Fettleworth said, and shouted for a bearer. He wanted his pudding now. 'I have also to consider my orders for the disposition of the brigade at Peshawar – the 114th's brigade, is it not? Now that the 114th has made up casualties, I see no reason to allow them to rest on their bottoms in cantonments and grow fat. They should be moved out towards the Chitral River again and held in readiness, Lakenham.'

'There is still the question of Brora, remember.'

'Yes, quite. But why do you single him out for mention at this moment?'

Lakenham answered patiently, 'Because, sir, he was the reason the brigade was withdrawn in the first place. Nothing has altered since then. Do you really consider it wise to reverse Calcutta's orders?'

'I'm not reversing Calcutta's orders, Lakenham, I am merely taking prudent precautions now the 114th are back to full strength. I spoke, did I not, of holding the brigade in readiness – I did not suggest an attack. It's a long march from Peshawar to Drosh if something should happen quickly. I must be ready for anything.' Bloody Francis dabbed at his lips with a napkin, then decided against pudding after all and called for the port he had bade his wife imagine they had reached earlier. He didn't stint himself in its imbibing; life was hard for a divisional commander on the North-West Frontier; life was one decision after another, plus privations when forced into the field. It was proper to take full advantage of one's comforts when possible. After his third glass of port Fettleworth had formulated the orders for Brigade, and he now passed them to his Chief of Staff for onward transmission to the Brigadier-General commanding in Peshawar: the 114th Highlanders together with their brigaded Indian battalions and their attached artillery were to be marched north-west for the Chitral as soon as possible and were to make camp some twenty miles south of Drosh to await further orders from Division.

'Ogilvie to be detached first?'

'I've already said that, Lakenham.'

By the time Ogilvie and Blaise-Willoughby had reached the small township of Garwar the day had been moving towards dark; and they entered in shadowy light, two itinerant traders from the east, men who would not be expected necessarily to know the ways of the people of Garwar and whose dialect, if it should differ in any respect, would not be remarked upon. Blaise-Willoughby carried rupees in a goatskin bag, concealed beneath his native garments but ready to be produced when the occasion demanded money. Circumspection would be used in its production, since evil men abounded, men well prepared to steal from hapless traders.

'They're an unprincipled bunch,' Blaise-Willoughby said as they made their way into the centre of the town, moving along in the stench from the open drain that ran down the middle of the street. 'But I don't need to tell you that, of course. Eyes and ears well open from now on, Ogilvie.'

They moved on; the place was crowded, filled with wild-looking men from the hills, Pathans from Afghanistan, Waziris and

Mahsuds from farther south, dirty men with *jezails* and long knives, men with penetrating eyes always on the watch for pickings. There were fat, sleek Hindus, men with a prosperous air about them and well protected by their bands of hired brigands who would ensure that their prosperity was not interfered with. These men would be the merchants, here in Garwar, no doubt, for the wife market, expectant of picking up bargains for re-sale in the more prosperous areas to the east...

Blaise-Willoughby gave Ogilvie a nudge, then whispered in his ear. 'Follow the Hindus just ahead there. They'll lead us in the right direction, I rather fancy.'

They kept behind the group of merchants. They went deeper into the town, along the narrow alleys where the hovels pressed close on either hand and more sharp eyes stared and ready hands fingered the blades of the knives and bayonets, or held the club that could shatter a man's skull like an eggshell. It was an eerie feeling and the temptation was strong to look continually over one's shoulder, but Ogilvie resisted this though he feared to feel at any moment the prick of steel in the back.

Ahead, the Hindu merchants with their

bodyguard turned into another alley running off to the left. Here they entered one of the dwellings and a door was shut behind them. Blaise-Willoughby didn't hesitate; moving on, he banged hard on the door as he had seen one of the merchants' bodyguard do. After a pause the door was opened and a tall, rangy man stood guarding it from just inside a dark passage at the end of which was light and sound, voices and the beat of erotic music.

'Who are you?' the man asked.

Blaise-Willoughby answered in Pushtu, 'I am a trader from Bhagalpur in Bengal, as is my friend.' He indicated Ogilvie. 'We come to bid for women.'

'You have money?'

'Yes, I have money.'

'Show it.'

Blaise-Willoughby brought the goatskin bag from under his clothing, and released the string at its neck. The man put a finger in amongst the rupees, and stirred. 'You may enter,' he said. He stood back, and the two officers went into the passage and the door was shut and bolted behind them. They moved towards the sound and light, the latter coming from many flares held aloft by the bidders in a sort of arena at the back of the hovel. The bidding had not in fact started yet; but there was an air of much expectancy amongst the audience as, amid the patter of tinny music, the flesh merchants and wife-seekers waited for the women to appear on a raised platform in the middle of the arena.

Four

The arena was small and closely packed; when the women appeared from one side, a passage had to be forced through for them by the tall native who had guarded the street door, now carrying a stout stick which he used freely to clear the bidders from his path.

The procession of women passed close to Ogilvie and Blaise-Willoughby. Ogilvie could almost feel their fear, their apprehension, their distaste for the proceedings that could decide the course of their future lives – in the majority of cases, that was; a handful were openly eyeing the men from above their veils, and seemed to be smiling.

65

They came in all shapes and sizes and what appeared to be all ages, though in all probability the oldest was not much more than twenty-five: India aged women fast, and especially those born to labour. There was a real stir of excitement now; the heat generated by the packed bodies seemed to increase almost feverishly, and the music grew louder, rising to a crescendo as the first of the women stepped up onto the platform and moved across it. One by one the women took up their places and faced their audience; dark-skinned hands reached up to feel ankles and squeeze thighs. The women submitted passively to the indignities; and after an interval filled with shouting and jostling for position, an imperious-looking Waziri, tall and richly clad, clambered onto the platform and faced the expectant dealers from the centre of the line of women. He started a long harangue, most of which Ogilvie was able to follow; he extolled the beauty and virtues of the women, suggesting that each and every one was a pearl without peer and worth any man's all. In their embrace happiness awaited the lucky purchaser, and all were well acquainted with the proper principles of unquestioning obedience and good housekeeping.

'They are faithful, frugal, and mindful of their master's possessions,' the Waziri asserted. 'If bought, the joy of heaven will be brought to the meanest dwelling as much as to the most splendid palace in all India. This I promise and guarantee.' He clapped his hands twice. 'Now we shall commence.'

The first woman was brought forward and her particular points brought to the attention of the bidders; then she was taken down from the platform and led through the crowd so that she could be assessed. Hands reached, eyes leered; she was young – no more than fourteen by Ogilvie's guess – and she was pretty, though with eyes as sad and fearful as the others who waited their turn. Led back to the platform, she was quickly knocked down for one hundred and ten rupees to one of the Hindu merchants who was not going to miss a bargain that would fetch very much more in the richer parts of India; the plain seekers after wives hadn't had a chance. Three more were as easily sold; the next two fared less well. The merchants made no bid at all, and the women went to two husbands, poor men with a nomadic look about them but with sufficient rupees saved up to buy the less favoured wares.

After this several more went to the merchants and then the really difficult end of the market was reached as the older women were paraded with their withered skins and sagging breasts, their hollow eyes and scraggy arms and unkempt hair. These went, if they went at all and some did not, to the wife seekers and went at dirt cheap prices; and there was much wailing and gnashing of teeth from the auctioneer who complained with bitterness that unless the women sold, and at proper prices, the supply would not be easy to maintain. Who, he asked loudly and with passion, would put himself to the bother and expense of bringing women into India for such ingratitude? It would become worth no-one's while. One of the merchants, heeding the warning, made a bid of a handful of annas for one of the less ill-visaged of the rejected women, and was allotted her. The future had to be considered, but he appeared much dissatisfied with his purchase.

It was while he was loudly venting his dissatisfaction that the sound of many horsemen was heard from the alley beyond the hovel, accompanied by shouts and the sharp crack of *jezails*. The noise in the arena died away; the tinny music at last stopped.

As it did so there came a thunderous banging at the door of the hovel and then the sound of splintering woodwork. The Waziri left the platform fast and panic broke out among the erstwhile bidders, who ran hither and thither in the greatest confusion. As they jostled one another, looking for a way out, riders crashed through the passageway from the alley, bent double over their horses' ears against the low ceiling. They were all in the gaudy, tattered uniforms of a private native army, and as they came through into the arena with lifted sabres held threateningly above the mob, Ogilvie was much shaken to see that the commanding figure of their leader was unmistakably that of Major Lord Brora, second-in-command of the Queen's Own Royal Strathspey. Brora clove through the panic-stricken bidders and rode for the platform with his sabre raised. A fat Hindu merchant was running across the stage and Brora used the flat of his blade to send the man down to the ground in a bleating heap, then pointed the sabre straight at the cowering women.

'Take the lot,' he shouted in Urdu to his native troop. 'They're all His Highness' property now and never mind who thinks he has bought them!' He waved the sabre over his head. 'Guard them well or you'll answer for it with your lives.'

The troop pressed forward, trampling the bidders under the hooves of their horses. Men screamed as they fell; blood and split heads were everywhere. There was no escape for anyone other than through the passageway, and that was guarded by a massive native trooper with his sabre ready to sever the head from the first body to seek escape.

'I'll be damned!' Blaise-Willoughby said later. Brora's native troop, once the women had been taken and laid across the pommels of the horses, had ridden out of the alley and thence out of Garwar, leaving the robbed purchasers behind to bemoan their lot. Those who had made no purchases left the premises hurriedly, and among them were the two British officers. 'What d'you make of all that, Ogilvie?'

'I don't know, and that's the truth. You?'

'Well, in the first place, it's the Rajah of Drosh, replenishing stock, obviously. Difficulties in the supply route, perhaps–'

'But surely he wouldn't grab back women he'd supplied himself, would he?'

Blaise-Willoughby, his native garments billowing out in a cold wind from the north and giving him a bat-like appearance, laughed harshly. 'I doubt it! He wouldn't be given any contract renewals if he did that. No – my guess is, Garwar never was His Highness' market at all and he's aiming to flatten it out as a rival.'

Ogilvie nodded. 'Yes, I suppose that holds water. What about Brora?'

'Brora remains the mystery. It's beginning to come together, though, isn't it? I mean, he's in it up to the neck now. I don't see any doubt at all.'

'He took a bloody great risk, didn't he? Anybody could have recognized him as we did ourselves!'

'I agree. But Brora's Brora, you've said so yourself. Brash ... no, that's not quite the word, *arrogant* to the point of complete belief in himself and a complete rejection of everyone else. He simply doesn't give a damn. He's become a renegade against the Raj and that's that.'

Ogilvie said, 'I can't believe it. It's not his style. There must be some other explanation. It's inconceivable that a British officer could go native as it were–'

'It's happened before now,' Blaise-Willoughby said. 'It's been hushed up – it was thought too nasty to be made public. Brora's

71

not the sort to be hushed up, unfortunately!' He paused. 'I know it's difficult to believe, Ogilvie, but what other explanation can there possibly be? I say again, I have no doubt at all – I'm very sorry, but there it is.'

'And that's what you intend to report to Division?'

'Yes. And the sooner we get there the better, Ogilvie, so let's start pushing the pace, shall we?'

In the early hours, by previous arrangements with the Adjutant who had instructed the sergeant of the barrack guard, Ogilvie and Blaise-Willoughby re-entered the Royal Strathspey's cantonment and divested themselves of their smelly native clothing in the guardroom, where the cast-off garments were put back in the Political Officer's saddlebags while he changed into his white suit.

'Waste not, want not,' he said.

'Do they get washed in the interval?'

'Probably not. Authenticity's more important than fastidiousness, and natives smell. Ready?'

'Almost.' Ogilvie was putting on his uniform; he had been greeted by a message from Andrew Black: orders had come in from Division. The brigade was under orders to march north and Captain Ogilvie was required to report the soonest possible to the Chief of Staff in Nowshera and to prepare for another absence from his regiment. He didn't care for the sound of that but there was nothing to be done about it and he could only assume that the Colonel would have been fully informed and had approved what seemed to be a fresh whim of Bloody Francis'. The Divisional Commander was full of whims and fancies, most of them highly dangerous to their victim, but usually with some useful purpose attached to them somewhere. The trick was to spot it; this time, for Ogilvie's money, it had to concern Brora or at any rate the Rajah of Drosh. He was right, he found when he and Blaise-Willoughby reported in at the Nowshera head-quarters after a fast ride from Peshawar.

Brigadier-General Lakenham took Ogilvie to the presence of Bloody Francis himself as the latter enjoyed a far from frugal breakfast. The Divisional Commander looked up from a plate of liver and bacon, such as normally followed his kedgeree before the toast-and-marmalade stage was reached.

'Ah, Ogilvie. Good morning, my boy.'

'Good morning, sir.'

Bloody Francis took a large mouthful and then said, 'Early to bed and early to rise – you'll have heard the saying, of course. Makes a man healthy, wealthy and wise.'

'Yes, sir.'

'You've breakfasted, of course?'

'No, sir.'

'Oh. Stupid of you, but never mind.' General Fettleworth wiped his lips with a starched napkin. 'I've sent for you so as to pass my orders personally. They're important and not to be misunderstood – I'd go so far as to say they're vital for the security of the Raj. Let damn Drosh get away with it and all the other buggers'll be at the same game, cocking snooks at His Excellency's authority – what?'

'Yes, sir.'

'Then there's that other business – damned unpleasant, that. I refer to your Major as you'll realize.'

'Yes, sir.'

'I've already seen Blaise-Willoughby. His report's quite damning. It's a dreadful thing to happen in my command, Ogilvie, and frankly I can't believe it *has* happened – oh, I know facts are facts but they're not always to be damn well *relied* on, y'know. I don't know if you follow?'

Ogilvie said, 'I think I do, sir. They can't always be taken at face value–'

'That's it, that's it exactly,' Bloody Francis said, sounding pleased. 'Everything has a reason behind it, I've always said that and I say it again now. I wish you to go upon a mission of discovery. I think you'll understand what I mean?'

'To discover what, sir?' Ogilvie asked.

Fettleworth frowned. 'I can't be precise. A good officer knows the mind of his Divisional Commander without being told, Captain Ogilvie.' He simmered for a while, tapping his fingers on the breakfast table. 'I want to know just what Drosh is up to, that's what! Is it to be a full-scale war upon the Raj, aided and abetted by that bugger in Kabul, or is it not? That sort of thing. I want to know his potential in terms of men and guns. So far my intelligence has not been as good as it might be. I believe you can do the job very well, my dear fellow, and as for Blaise-Willoughby, for one thing he's likely to be known to that bloody little Rajah and for another I need him here. As a regimental officer, you're not so likely to be known.'

'I shall be known to Lord Brora, sir.'

Fettleworth glared and blew up the trailing

75

ends of his white moustache. 'Mean to say you're asking not to be sent, Ogilvie?'

'No, sir. I was simply pointing out a fact that–'

'Facts again,' Fettleworth said disagreeably. 'However, I take your point. My Chief of Staff has already mentioned it, as it happens, and I have dealt with it and solved it. You'll not actually enter the palace, which you'd find hard to do in any case – too damned slow, trying to ingratiate yourself with the Rajah's major domo so as to be given a job as a scullion or something.' Bloody Francis rasped at his cheeks with his hand. 'No, you'll enter the area of Drosh as an Afghan who's crossed the Frontier with the object of picking up information for the Amir about the Rajah's plans against the Raj, and you'll drop suggestions that the Amir in Kabul is having second thoughts about marching his damned brigands and bandits in support. That should put a few straws into the wind, I fancy! You must watch the way those straws are blown, Ogilvie. But remember your first duty is to find out what Brora's up to. That's the vital part.'

'Yes, sir. How should I go about that, sir?'

Fettleworth frowned. 'Damn it, I'm your

General! It's not for me to itemize every blasted thing, Ogilvie. Use your initiative for God's sake!'

The 114th's Brigade moved out from Peshawar during that morning, Lord Dornoch, as the senior colonel, riding with Brigadier-General Shaw in the lead behind the battalion pipes and drums. The Regimental Sergeant-Major, as he marched up the column of Scots, critically eyeing the set of kilts and the tightness of the belts and cross-belts of the men's field equipment, found the words of the pipers' tune running through his head and forcing him to hum in time to them:

Oh, the thistle o' Scotland was famous of auld
Wi' its toorie snod and its bristles sae bauld;
'Tis the badge o' my country, it's aye dear tae me,
And the thocht o' them baith brings the tear tae my e'e.

Cunningham grinned to himself; not many Highlanders gave way to tears, but the sentiment was right enough. He marched on, thinking of Scotland and the depot at Invermore which he hadn't seen for years past. There was a deep longing in him to see again his own mountains and the blue lochs, the heather and the rowan, and to walk through the glens of his childhood, well remembered in all their detail, though in all truth it would not be the same without his wife. Cunningham had never recovered from the blow of her murder in the Royal Strathspey's own cantonment; to that extent his life was over, and the regiment was all that was left. He would not wish to go back to Scotland without it, however deep his love for the highlands; but time went on and unless the Colonel could manage to extend his service beyond the norm then retirement and a pension would loom. Cunningham pushed down such thoughts, firmly: he had a few years left yet and there was still a job to be done. Currently it was back towards Drosh again, and the dangerous mountain passes beneath the burning Indian sun ... coming up in rear of B Company the Regimental Sergeant-Major watched the tall figure of Private Campbell marching as though he were parading past the Queen at the Horse Guards at the Trooping the Colour, or beating retreat in the forecourt of

Buckingham Palace. Cunningham pulled at his moustache. The man was putting the Scots to shame at the moment, but a pound to a penny he'd wilt before the rest of the battalion did. Gentlemen rankers ... Cunningham shook his head; it was a dog's life until they'd made it and then, he supposed, it all seemed worth while.

Cunningham was hailed by the Adjutant, riding down the column from the van.

'Mr Cunningham!'

'Sir!' The RSM saluted.

'The order has not yet been passed to march at ease, Mr Cunningham.'

'No, sir.'

'Then kindly have words with the colour-sar'nts. There is a lack of precision in the set of the helmets, and I've noticed two men in A Company with their tunic collars loosened. Take their names, if you please, Sar'nt-Major.'

'Very good, sir.'

Captain Black rode on towards the rear, eyes searching, dark jowls giving him a perpetual scowl. Cunningham sighed: smartness was important and any lack of it reflected upon himself, but Black was forever nit-picking and in all truth it would take a spirit-level to detect any disparity in the angles of the Wolseley helmets. Loosened collars – that was a different matter. Until the order came from the Brigadier-General to march at ease collar bands must be kept tight even if the sweat choked the wearers. Cunningham quickened his pace and had words with the Colour-Sergeant of the offending company, and names were duly taken. On return to cantonments, two Scots would face extra drill and fatigues.

Five

Ogilvie, mounted in his disguise as a Pathan tribesman out of Afghanistan, rode out from the British garrison at Mardan to the north of the Brigade's initial westward advance from Peshawar; whilst the brigade had been upon that westerly route Ogilvie had ridden in uniform as far as Mardan, where the transformation had been made. By the time the battalions had turned for the north, he had outflanked them and was across their line of advance, lying low for the time being in the hills to the west, between Afghanistan and the lands of Drosh. The brigade, he had been informed in Nowshera, was under orders to halt and go into camp twenty miles south of the palace and was to wait there in readiness for further orders. In the meantime His Highness was to be left in peace.

Much would depend upon what Ogilvie was able to find out, and he must lose no time. To delay would in any case be dangerous in a personal sense: the dye that, applied in Mardan, stained his skin more permanently than that applied in cantonments for his venture into the wife market, would wear off before many days had passed.

From the hills, he rode down fast towards the city of Drosh and was soon in its teeming alleys, mean, sordid and smelly against the splendid backdrop of nature. He rode along, arrogant as any wild Pathan would be amongst townspeople, seeking out the hovel of a seller of opium, a man recommended to him by Major Blaise-Willoughby before he had left Nowshera.

'Prasad Diwaker,' Blaise-Willoughby had said, 'is a man of many parts but chiefly opium. He's useful so long as there are rupees in it – not to be trusted an inch, of course, but who is, in India? The point is, he usually knows everything that's going on in

Drosh and he should be a good starting off point.'

'What are his loyalties, Major?'

'Himself,' Blaise-Willoughby said. 'He's helped the Raj before now, and he's also done the opposite. Again, I refer you to rupees. Take plenty with you – in fact, I'll see to the requisition myself and get some dynamite put under the paymaster. There's one other point you may find useful: Prasad Diwaker, though he wouldn't say so in public, has no love for His Highness, none at all. The little bugger–'

'Which little bugger?'

Blaise-Willoughby grinned. 'His Highness. Prasad Diwaker's daughters, three of them, were taken a few years ago by the Rajah for his harem. They've since died ... the old man's been saved a good deal of expense, but he's still bitter. He's said to have loved them. You might just bear it in mind.'

Riding the alleys of Drosh, Ogilvie thought about Blaise-Willoughby's words. Probably few people in the city had much love for the Rajah, and that, too, might be worth bearing in mind.

He rode on, pushing through the crowds, making to Blaise-Willoughby's directions for the Street of the Opium Sellers under the sun's ferocious heat that was to bring to a head all the smells of the over-populated city. There seemed scarcely room to move; men and women and children jostled, some of them relieved themselves in the open sewer or against the walls of the dwellings, others slept at full stretch in the shadows, risking being walked upon by the crowds or worried by the roaming pariah dogs with their mangy fur and capacity to spread disease. Over all there was a curious sense of unease, of fear, of a constant looking over the shoulder in case trouble should come. It was an emanation of something evil, no doubt originating from the palace that dominated the city from the crest of a hill and from behind high mud walls and guarded gateways. Every one of the city's inhabitants, Ogilvie felt, lived in terror of the grasping hand of one of the Rajah's soldiers, the grasp that could lead to the palace dungeons or the executioner's blade.

Ogilvie turned into the Street of the Opium Sellers; somewhere the weed was being smoked – the smell was pervasive, sickly. Human degradation lurked behind the dirty, once-white walls; no doubt in the fumes of the poppy the Rajah and his machinations could be forgotten as the fantasies whirled through the drugged minds, and a kind of heaven was enjoyed while the pipe lasted. It was understandable, and it was manna to the sellers.

Prasad Diwaker's establishment was right at the end of the alley, right on the outskirts of the town to the east, with rocky country beyond leading clear to the distant hills fringing the remote land of Kashmir. Finding it, Ogilvie dismounted and tethered his horse and, clutching his *jezail* and feeling the bullet-laden bandoliers bumping his chest through his filthy garment, bent his body to enter a dark room leading straight off the street. At first he could make out nothing; then, as his eyes grew accustomed to the gloom, he saw a man sitting cross-legged on the bare earth floor, staring at him curiously. He was a man of many years, bent and frail.

'What do you want?' this ancient asked creakily, speaking in halting Pushtu as he recognized a supposed Afghan. 'Who are you?'

'I am Amanullah Sarabi. You are Prasad Diwaker?'

'I am he. How do you know this?'

'In Kabul you are spoken of. Prasad Diwaker, the seller of opium is well known to me by name.'

'You come for opium, Amanullah Sarabi?'

'No. I do not come for opium.'

'Then for what do you come?'

Ogilvie said, 'In Kabul I was told that you would be a safe person to confide in, and that you would deliver a message to the Rajah's palace – and that afterwards you would prove a friendly person who would give me lodging for a consideration.'

'Who told you this, Amanullah Sarabi?'

'Many persons in the confidence of the Amir, from whom I come.'

'The Amir?' Prasad Diwaker drew in a sharp breath. 'The Amir himself?'

Ogilvie nodded. 'I am his personal messenger, with most important tidings for His Highness Rajah Mohan Singh.'

Prasad Diwaker considered this information for some while, still staring through the gloom at Ogilvie. Then he said, 'You would wish your business to be conducted in more privacy than is possible in my poor shop, I do not doubt. Come.'

In the van of the British advance away to the south, Brigadier-General Shaw lifted his right arm, then brought it down sharply. Behind him the long column came to a halt;

the order was passed by the Brigade Major to fall out. There would be a quarter of an hour's rest and smoke before camp was made: the brigade was now in its position as ordered by Bloody Francis and as yet no-one knew for how long they would be expected to remain, or when the time would come for action. There was any amount of speculation as the men took their ease, and the pipes were lit. As they sprawled on the hard, sun-dried ground under the care of the posted picquets, the Regimental Sergeant-Major was once again called by Captain Black.

'Sir!'

'There is to be full alertness, Mr Cunningham. The Brigadier-General thinks the Rajah may send out probes and may seek a parley when the word reaches him that we're here – as of course it will and no doubt has already. There's to be no mistakes made as between the Rajah's army and any stray Pathan bandits that may be seen. Do you understand me?'

'Aye, sir. No trigger-happiness from the picquets.'

'Nor on the part of the camp guard either, Mr Cunningham. Brigade's to be informed at once of any sightings and no action of any sort is to be taken other than on the Brigadier-General's order.' Black paused, and pulled at his moustache. 'The situation promises to be a tricky one, and delicate.'

'I understand, sir.' No mention was made of Lord Brora's presence in Drosh, but Cunningham knew that that presence was the reason behind the delicacy. Delicate was scarcely the word; there could be the worst scandal ever to strike the Raj and the British Army in India, for all anyone could tell, once Lord Brora came as it were into the open. Cunningham's heart was heavy as the Adjutant rode back up the resting column, his horse's hooves kicking up the dust along the track. Scandal, once it attached itself to a regiment, had a habit of sticking for a long while. When the orders came for camp to be made the men were brought to their feet by the colour-sergeants and the tents were shaken out from the transport wagons and the mule-train; Cunningham, with the Regimental Quartermaster Sergeant, watched critically as the operation proceeded; and when the lines were set up they walked along checking distances between tents and ensuring that all guys were taut. The commissariat and the camp followers were quartered at the southern end of the en-

campment, while the gunners of the attached mountain batteries assembled their guns
from the backs of the mules and wheeled
them into position on the flanks. At the
northern end, facing towards Drosh, stood
the battalion Maxims.

Making his own check of B Company's
lines, Colour-Sergeant MacTrease found
Private Campbell staring towards the mountains to the north, and called to him.

Campbell snapped to attention and turned
smartly. 'Colour-Sar'nt!'

'Nothing to do but stand and gawp, is that
it?'

'I'm sorry, Colour-Sar'nt.'

A grin lurked round MacTrease's mouth.
'No excuse to offer, eh?'

'No, Colour-Sar'nt.'

'That's better than coming up with something bloody daft, anyway. Have you ever
made camp before?'

'Only on manoeuvres, Colour-Sar'nt–'

'Salisbury Plain?'

'Yes. I–'

'All spit and polish, no doubt. You'll find it
different out here on the Frontier, laddie.
We're on active service, not manoeuvres.
You'll keep your wits about you and your
rifle handy.' MacTrease paused, looking

88

Campbell up and down. 'I take it, when you were with the Coldstream, you had the status of Trained Soldier?'

Campbell nodded. 'Yes, Colour-Sar'nt.'

'And entitled to a wee bit of respect from the recruits. Maybe that'll stand you in good stead, who knows? All right, Campbell, carry on now.'

MacTrease walked away. He was anticipatory of action; action was ever just round the corner along the North-West Frontier but he felt in his bones that something really big was stirring this time, something much bigger than an ambush or simple patrol activity; and large-scale action brought the inevitability of heavy casualties. Some of the NCOs would be among those casualties, and would need to be replaced. It was part of a colour-sergeant's duty to have his recommendations ready, and Private Campbell looked as though he was shaping up well enough to be considered for lance. You couldn't discount the Guards training.

Ogilvie had followed Prasad Diwaker through a bead-curtained doorway into a passage. Prasad Diwaker led the way through into a courtyard, pushing open a stout door, and from the courtyard into a low building on its far side. Here there was a window that looked out upon the Rajah's palace-fortress, rising high upon its hilltop beneath a clear sky. Ogilvie moved for this window and looked out; Prasad Diwaker came to his side and stood for a few moments, also looking across at the palace. Then he said, 'The tidings that you have for His Highness, Amanullah Sarabi.'

'Yes?'

'Can you not take the news to him yourself?' There was a dry chuckle. 'Or do you fear the fate that is said to be visited upon the bearer of tidings ... if the tidings are bad ones?'

'I have not said the tidings are bad, Prasad Diwaker, and I fear nothing – but I am not so foolish as to walk into the lion's den when I have no need to do so.'

'Which is the same thing in different words,' the opium dealer said with another chuckle. 'From this I deduce that in fact the news will not be to His Highness' liking. This is so?'

Ogilvie inclined his head. 'It is indeed so, Prasad Diwaker. The news is that the Amir in Kabul has changed his mind. He will not now send his armies to assist Rajah Mohan Singh against the Raj.'

'And his reason?'

'Rajah Mohan Singh has cheated him over monies deriving from the trade in women.'

Prasad Diwaker nodded but for some moments offered no comment. Then he asked, 'You wish me to deliver this message to the palace, Amanullah Sarabi?'

'It would be a favour if you were to arrange for this. Also to make it understood that I, the messenger, have already gone back across the hills into my own country.'

'Which – am I to understand – you will not in fact have done?'

Ogilvie smiled. 'You are a man of much perception, Prasad Diwaker! I ask that you permit me shelter and lodging in your house, in return of course for payment, so that in due time I may return to Kabul and inform the Amir of the effect of his change of mind upon Rajah Mohan Singh and his plans for the future.'

'Which effect you will obtain by observation?'

'And by the use of my ears and yours also, Prasad Diwaker. When I return to Kabul, the Amir will decide upon *his* plans for the future, and if Rajah Mohan Singh has not shown signs of mending his ways, the Amir may decide to force such mending upon

91

him.'

Prasad Diwaker pursed his lips. 'Then much trouble will come to Drosh.'

'If the Amir should attack, yes. But wars are always good for those who know how to profit by them, Prasad Diwaker, is this not so?'

The Indian nodded. 'Indeed it can be so.' He paused in thought for a long time, staring towards the grim-looking palace and fingering his chin. Calculations were being made and risks assessed and balanced against the possible advantages and gains, not all of them financial: there was the consideration that Prasad Diwaker's heart was filled with hatred for the tyrant Mohan Singh who had deprived him of his daughters. After his deliberations Prasad Diwaker said, 'You shall lodge here, Amanullah Sarabi. Money will be discussed first. The message will be delivered to the palace, but not by myself. I shall make certain arrangements and neither my name nor yours will be spoken. This is agreed?'

Ogilvie nodded. 'It is agreed. There is one more favour I have to ask of you, Prasad Diwaker.'

'Ask, then.'

Ogilvie said, 'There are rumours in Kabul

that a British officer is residing in the palace of Mohan Singh.'

Prasad Diwaker rocked gently back and forth on his heels. 'So: if there is, then what, Amanullah Sarabi?'

'It is possible that His Highness is, shall we say, more friendly towards the Raj than has been thought in the past – and thought, moreover, in Kabul.'

'Thought by the Amir?'

'Exactly so.'

'And this, perhaps, is why the Amir is withdrawing his support for Rajah Mohan Singh?'

'Perhaps. I am but the poor messenger. I am not party to the decisions of the Amir.' Ogilvie paused, watching the wily face of Prasad Diwaker closely. 'Tell me, Prasad Diwaker: do you know anything of this British officer?'

'Nothing.' The answer was prompt, dismissive. 'I do not know even if he is residing in the palace or not, I do not know if he exists–'

'Yet you are said to have long ears and all-seeing eyes.'

Prasad Diwaker lifted his shoulders and the palms of his hands. 'If that is what is said of me, then perhaps there is truth in the saying, but of this British officer I know nothing and I can answer no questions concerning him. Your message will be delivered to the palace and that is all I can offer. Now we shall discuss the provision of payment.' The eyes glittered with greed. 'You bring rupees, Amanullah Sarabi?'

'Yes. I bring also the means of protecting them.' Ogilvie lifted his *jezail*, bringing the butt down to his right thigh so that the tip of the snaky bayonet was presented to the Indian; but smiled placatingly as he did so.

'You do not trust me?' Prasad Diwaker asked, lifting his eyebrows.

'Like my own brother. But there will be those that cannot be trusted, and I shall guard my rupees with my life.'

'You are a prudent man,' Prasad Diwaker observed; and thereafter much haggling took place, a sum being grudgingly agreed after some half-hour, this sum to cover the inconvenience and out-of-pocket expense to which Prasad Diwaker would be put in having the message conveyed to His Highness, and also to cover a week's lodging in his house for the Amir's emissary.

The brief twilight ended and the dusk came down over the British encampment. Supper had been provided by the field kitchens, and now the soldiers turned in for the night, to sleep under the care of the posted picquets – well distanced to give as much alarm as possible should an attack come – and under the camp guard commanded by a sergeant and provided, on this first night, by the 114th Highlanders. Sergeant MacKay, next to Colour-Sergeant MacTrease on B Company's seniority list, took the first duty, from eight p.m. to midnight. He made constant rounds of the perimeter, visiting each sentry and keeping his own ears a-flap and his eyes busy as the rising moon threw down shadows from the hills, those points of danger to all British forces operating alone the Frontier.

The night was a very silent one, the intense quiet broken only occasionally by the scurry of small animals, the call of a night bird and the rattle of rifle-slings and field equipment as the sentries marched their posts.

Nothing else: no alarms or excursions from the picquets along the peaks. Sergeant MacKay reached the post patrolled by Private Campbell and had words with him.

'Good experience for you, Campbell,' MacKay observed, noting in the bright moonlight the man's excellent turn-out, not a strap out of place, the boots polished like mirrors, the set of tunic and kilt exactly right. 'How do you find India so far, eh?'

'Interesting, Sar'nt.'

'Interesting?' MacKay gave a somewhat hollow laugh. 'I've another name for the bloody place, but no matter. I've been out here a while and maybe I'm soured.' He paused, lifting his chin and easing his neck in the tunic-collar, wondering at his own affability ... he wouldn't stop for a yarn with many privates, for it could be bad for discipline, but it couldn't be denied there was something intriguing about a gentleman ranker. MacKay had heard of them but until now had never met one in the flesh, and it was a curious experience, not least to hear the voice of a gentleman coming from beneath a private's headgear and addressing him with respect and an element of fear. Talk about a reversal of fortune! In other circumstances he, Sergeant MacKay of the 114th Highlanders, the Queen's Own Royal Strathspey, might well be this gentleman's groom or ghillie; rumour had it that his father had money enough. To many it would be a temptation to haze and harry the gentleman and watch him hop to the shouts of the "below stairs" minions as it were, but

MacKay was a good NCO and as such would do nothing of the sort. Indeed he wished Campbell luck and said so.

'I'll hope you'll make the officers' mess, laddie,' he said. 'What you're doing takes guts.'

'Thank you, Sar'nt. I don't see it that way myself, though. I just want to get ahead in the army.'

MacKay nodded. 'They'll not commission you in the 114th, of course.'

'No, Sar'nt. But I hope it'll be another highland regiment. Camerons, Seaforths, Black Watch, Gordons, Argyll and Sutherland, Highland Light Infantry ... I'd be proud to join any of them. As a matter of fact–' Campbell broke off suddenly and stared along the track coming down from the north, stared towards the blackness of a defile that lay ahead between great sheer sides of rock. 'Sar'nt, I believe there's a force coming through – the moon's reflecting from bayonets, I fancy–'

MacKay turned about sharply and after one look lost no time. 'Jesus, the bloody picquets must be asleep!' he said, and put a whistle to his lips. He blew three long blasts, then clapped Campbell on the shoulder. 'Well done, laddie,' he said. He doubled away, shouting the men awake as he ran, making for the Brigade tent. The Brigade Commander was already pulling on his tunic and all along the lines men were turning out under the colour-sergeants and junior NCOs, their rifles in their hands, to await orders to repel what now looked like an attack in strength. A great horde of native cavalry was storming down from out of the mouth of the defile, yelling and screaming now that they had clearly been seen. The bugles blew over the encampment, Brigade's order to man the perimeter and withdraw the picquets and extended sentries within the camp. As the bolts of the rifles were worked to send the first bullets up the spouts, and as the Maxims and mountain batteries wheeled into position for action, a hail of carbine fire came from the native force and the moon glinted down evilly on the blades of the cavalry sabres borne by the Rajah's officers.

Six

Prasad Diwaker was back within a couple of hours and there was a wariness in his expression as he rejoined Ogilvie. He said, 'The message has been delivered, Amanullah Sarabi.'

'I am grateful. So will the Amir be grateful.'

'Yes. I trust he will continue so to be.'

Ogilvie's eyes narrowed. 'What do you mean by that?'

'I am forced into that which I do not wish to do, Amanullah Sarabi, and I am most sorry.'

'I do not understand.'

'His Highness insists upon words with you.'

'I have said—'

'Yes, yes. This I know. But I am powerless. You must understand that if I do not accede to the commands of His Highness, it will go ill for me. My life would be in danger.'

'Or your purse,' Ogilvie snapped, feeling a shaft of fear run along his spine. 'My orders to you were that you should say I was already on my way back into Afghanistan. That would have been your excuse for not finding me when the Rajah ordered you to do so. Your greed—'

'A man must live, Amanullah Sarabi, and must be allowed to live without fear—'

'As a rat, you mean!' Ogilvie brought up his *jezail*, threateningly. 'I have a mind to shoot you here and now, on behalf of my master, the Amir in Kabul—' He broke off. Prasad Diwaker had clapped his hands and whilst doing so had backed away to the door into the courtyard. As he reached it, four armed men entered. British Army pattern Lee Enfields – stolen, obviously from one of the armouries of the Raj – stared Ogilvie in the face. The men closed in. Ogilvie's finger tightened on the trigger of his *jezail* but the men were a shade too fast for him; as he fired the barrel of the weapon was seized and jerked upwards with immense strength. The bullet smacked into the woodwork around the door and the *jezail* was wrenched from Ogilvie's grip. A rifle-butt took him across the side of the head, painfully, and he went down gasping. A kick was aimed at his side, landing with immense force. Prasad Diwaker watched, wringing his hands: more rupees might yet have been mulcted from the Pathan had he been allowed a little more time. As it happened, the Indian had no time left to him at all. One of the rifles came up at a word from the men's leader, aimed at Prasad Diwaker. The trigger was squeezed. The Indian, a look of comical and immense surprise on his greedy face, was almost disembowelled by the shot at close range. There was a laugh from the men as he squirmed for a moment in agony, then died.

Speaking in Pushtu, the leader said, 'Now come, Amanullah Sarabi. His Highness demands apologies from the Amir in Kabul, and demands also that promises be met.'

He reached down and dragged Ogilvie to his feet. There was a ray of hope, perhaps, if a slim one: it appeared to Ogilvie that he was being taken at face value, as a genuine Pathan. Inside the Rajah's palace that would be harder to keep up, and there was the enigma of Lord Brora, but there was yet hope.

Thanks to Private Campbell's vigilance, the attack, though still holding some of the element of surprise, had been shorn of its totality as such. The first wave of firing caused many casualties in the British lines, but the return fire was swift and accurate and native bodies were seen to fall from the horses in large numbers as the cavalry thundered past on both flanks, firing as they rode. It was an attack similar to those carried out by American Indians on the wagon trains of the westward-pressing pioneer days.

Dornoch, cursing the absence of his second-in-command who was at his best in action, was called to Brigade by the Brigadier-General's runner. He reported at the double, saluting as he halted.

'Sir?'

Brigadier-General Shaw turned. 'Ah, Dornoch. The men are doing splendidly. I've a feeling we're going to beat off this attack though our casualties will probably be heavy enough. Thing is, what do we do afterwards?' He paused. 'Stay put, or follow through?'

'The orders from Divison—'

'Yes, I know what Fettleworth's orders were, but I'm on the spot and he isn't.' The Brigade Commander wiped sweat from his face; the night was cold enough, but the nervous energy expended during an action tended to bring out the sweat. 'If there's to be continual attack, we could be worn down by sheer attrition. Drosh will have any God's amount of reserves – this isn't his entire bloody army, Dornoch!'

'True. Well, I'd always sooner fight back than wait to be brought to action in some-one else's time!'

'My feelings exactly, Dornoch. And that's what I propose to do. The moment the natives show signs of pulling out, the brig-ade will move to close the defile and finish off as many of the buggers as possible. After that, we shall strike camp and march through towards Drosh.' The Brigadier-General paused. 'I'm not unmindful of the orders from Division, but I think the situa-tion's changed. Fettleworth didn't appear to envisage an attack upon us – that makes all the difference. What d'you think, Dornoch?'

'I agree with you, sir.'

'Good!' The Brigadier-General gave a nod, and Dornoch ran back to rejoin his battal-ion. The firing was heavy still, the natives yelling like madmen as they galloped around the camp's perimeter, but the attack was beginning already to lose its momentum. The native losses were very heavy; the Maxims were having a field day, stuttering into the horsemen as they passed by and bringing them down in screaming swathes. Dornoch, standing like a rock on a piece of rising ground where he could be seen clearly by his battalion in the moonlight, noted some individual acts of bravery on the part of his Scots. Sergeant MacKay died with a sabre-cut across his neck when, during a native attempt to hack through the perimeter, he interposed himself between the Regimental Sergeant-Major and a native horseman. A lance-corporal ran through heavy fire to the assistance of the Surgeon Major, who was attending to the wounded, when another attempt at penetration was made in the northern sector. Private Campbell, only so very recently joined, was pumping away with his rifle, doggedly, in spite of the blood that stained his khaki-drill tunic. Dornoch's eye was on him when suddenly he made a dash out from the perimeter, his bayoneted rifle raised high above his head – Dornoch believed he had run out of ammunition – and carried out a bayonet attack on a native officer, the man who appeared to be the leader of the Rajah's force. As Campbell approached he brought his rifle down, then lunged upwards into the native's stomach. It could not have been done better by any drill-sergeant of the Guards. The man fell, to have his body dragged behind his horse by a trapped foot, and Campbell, dodging bullets and sabres, ran back inside the perimeter.

There was a shout from the Brigadier-General, and then the bugle sounded. Dornoch ran for Brigade, where he was joined by the Colonels of the attached battalions, both of them native units of the Indian Army. The Brigadier-General had noted a wavering in the attackers as their leader fell. He said, 'This is our chance, gentlemen.' He waved an arm towards the south. 'You see? They're re-forming down there, presumably to cut off our retreat route – but we're not going that way! We break off action at once, gentlemen, and move as fast as we know how for the mouth of the defile, and form up behind the guns. Get your men on the move right away.'

The Colonels dispersed; again the bugles blew and the orders were shouted to get the men moving out northwards. No time was lost; they ran like lunatics while the mountain batteries wheeled across the rear of the advance and pumped shells into the native force, holding them at bay for long enough to allow the infantry to reach the defile. Then they began pulling back, firing still. Now the mouth of the defile was closed. Colour-Sergeant MacTrease, breathing heavily, found the Regimental Sergeant-Major alongside him. He said, 'The buggers'll find another way round rather than face us, that's my guess.'

Cunningham shook his head. 'I remember these parts ... when the battalion relieved Ford Gazai. There is no other way to Drosh.'

MacTrease looked around, sucking his teeth. That was probably true; the mountains were sheer, no hope of climbing them. To get round them would very likely mean a drop south towards the road running from Peshawar to the Khyber Pass, and down there they would risk running slap into a British patrol with reinforcements handily placed to be contacted by a mounted runner. MacTrease spat on his hands and looked anticipatory: the fight now would be to the finish.

Ogilvie had been placed upon his own horse, his hands tied behind his back. A rope had been looped over his shoulders and hauled taut around him, the other end held by one of the Rajah's men riding in rear. Another man rode ahead and the other two placed themselves on Ogilvie's flanks. They moved away from the Street of the Opium Sellers, climbing a steep alley that led to the walls of the palace. The ride was a painful one; Ogilvie was feeling the effects both of the rifle-butt and the kick in his side. The pain in his side came with every movement of the horse, and he felt the sweat pour from his body as he compressed his lips against any sound of distress. As the riders approached the palace the track grew steeper and more rutted. They were let through a guarded gateway, a vast metal-studded door being opened to admit them as they were observed from a spy hole, then closed behind them with a doomful-sounding thud. The way climbed still; the walls were high and cut off all sight of the town below, but the great palace itself was set higher still, brooding with a sense of evil and cruelty that seemed to stretch back into past centuries of terror and torment for its prisoners and, no doubt, for all the dependent townspeople of Drosh. The palace seemed to have a myriad of tall towers that probed white into the blue sky, rearing above the battlemented roofs of the lower work which itself was immense and must contain hundreds of apartments. In the palace of Drosh, all the residences of the Queen-Empress could be fitted comfortably and still leave ample space to spare for the Rajah and his retinue, his servants, his concubines, his many wives, his officers of state of which there would be many for His Highness ruled over vast territories and many hundreds of thousands of people, all of whom paid him tribute of one sort or another.

Ogilvie was led towards the main entry to the palace and as he reached the bottom of a long flight of marble steps, the leading-rope was cast loose and he was ordered to dismount.

He did so, stiffly, wincing with pain. The boot had been heavy, and had broken the skin, and his ribs were sore.

He was prodded up the steps ahead of the bayonets on the Lee Enfields. At the top he entered a magnificent hall, a great space guarded at its door by four men of the Rajah's army in colourful but tinsel-looking uniforms. Never mind his enormous wealth: His Highness was a frugal man when it came to spending on his menials, and the uniforms had seen better days. The weapons, however, looked serviceable enough though the steel of the bayonets and the knives was rusty.

Ogilvie looked around the hall, finding it

more impressive than any native ruler's palace he had yet seen. Tall columns of marble rose to a vaulted ceiling richly and erotically decorated in gold and silver and what looked like precious stones – the green of emeralds, the rich red of rubies, the sparkle of great diamonds interspersed with the lesser stones such as topaz and onyx, jet and tourmaline. From somewhere came music, thin and tinny. The floor was of marble like the columns, with Persian rugs spread at intervals. From the centre of the northern side a wide staircase rose to a half landing, twisting up again from either hand; again there was much marble, overlaid this time with a thick carpet of peacock blue, while the banisters appeared to be of solid gold with tigers' heads of silver at their ends. The air was filled with the heady smell of spices, ones that Ogilvie was unable to identify, but their purpose was obvious enough: from beneath them came other smells that they had not quite overlaid, the smells of stale food, of cooking, of unwashed bodies and of drains or the lack of them.

The bayonets moved Ogilvie to the left, where another splendid apartment opened off the great hall. From here was coming chatter, the light voices of many women, and laughter that rippled through now and again as Ogilvie approached. The sound was stilled as he went through the doorway, and heads were turned towards him and his wild-looking escort: he could feel, almost as a physical force, the effect of the staring eyes. Looking to his right, he saw His Highness Rajah Mohan Singh seated upon a golden, silk-cushioned throne with two women at his feet. Beside him, some standing, some sitting, were some of his principal aides. A motley bunch of warlike men and fat, paunchy men with the look of office *wallahs* – and a white man wearing a white silk suit: Major Lord Brora of the 114th Highlanders. Brora stared at the approaching procession, head held back disdainfully, nose in the air, complete with all the arrogance that he was accustomed to display in cantonments at Peshawar. Ogilvie's fear of recognition – and his abounding curiosity as to what on earth Brora could be doing in Drosh – increased. Brora most certainly had no aspect of being in the palace under any kind of duress.

'They're coming in now,' Dornoch said. He raised his voice. 'Captain Black?'

'Colonel?'

'Remember the Major's no longer with us.'

'I shall remember, Colonel.' Black's voice was solemn; he had taken Dornoch's meaning. If the Colonel should die, command of the battalion would devolve upon himself. The Brigadier-General regarded it as important that the Rajah of Drosh should be taught a lesson once and for all and never mind Division or even Calcutta. The politicians, and often enough the generals well behind the lines, were frequently out of touch with the reality of the field. Brigadier-General Shaw was a man of action and decision and he believed that the Rajah would be given pause by an extermination of his force and would be found amenable enough after the arrival outside his palace of a brigade not only still in being but shortly to be reinforced from Nowshera – if General Fettleworth didn't decide to be awkward. In the absence of the field telegraph – whose wires, rolled out behind the brigade's advance, had been cut by bandits as was usually the case with the field telegraph – four mounted runners had been detailed to ride south with Shaw's request for reinforcements the moment the native force had been engaged by the artillery, their preoccupation giving the runners the chance to ride and

111

outflank them. Andrew Black lifted his field glasses: he could hear the pounding hooves of the cavalry and the yells of the native horsemen. The carbines were already firing; bullets snicked off the rock sides and off the boulders being used as cover by the Scots and the brigaded Indian Army units. No return fire was ordered yet; let the buggers waste their ammunition, had been the Brigadier-General's dictum.

When the order did come, it was a shock discharge and immediately effective: every man fired in unison from his cover, the Maxims opened, and, positioned on the flanks of the defile's mouth, the mountain batteries sent their shells screaming point-blank into the cavalry charge. It was nothing less than slaughter: there was pandemonium as men and horses crashed before the tremendous barrage of fire, as shells exploding in orange flame to shatter bodies, tear off arms and legs and disembowel stomachs. The awesome stench, sharp and acrid, of gunsmoke drifted over the appalling scene, stark and clear beneath the moon's light. As the native force reeled back the guns pursued them until they had scattered out of effective range. Advantage was taken of a lull to refill the bandoliers and pass more ammunition to the Maxims and the mountain artillery. Then the Rajah's men were seen to be re-grouping and coming in once more, an act of senseless bravery. Then something appeared to go wrong: there were shouted orders faintly heard, and the field glasses noted a turning aside in the attack. It was Cunningham who first saw what was happening and interpreted it.

'They're heading for the camp! The buggers mean to attack the wounded!' Cunningham was on his feet now, waving his revolver. He had already moved out from cover and was running for the camp when the order came down by the bugle from Brigade: the battalions were to advance. Behind the 114th's RSM the men doubled out, running hell for leather and moving very fast, firing as they ran. The Maxims and the guns moved forward more slowly, waiting their chance to open: they could not fire upon the camp with its wounded men. After a hasty word with the Brigadier-General, Dornoch passed orders via Black to his Company Commanders to take their men towards the west flank; one of the native battalions was to double easterly while the other covered the northern sector of the perimeter. The idea was to sweep the camp and squeeze the Rajah's troops out via the southern sector, when they would come under the fire of the heavy guns, now ordered to trundle to the south as fast as they could manage, a half battery being left behind in case the natives should attempt to cut and run through the defile for home.

They had just pounded up to the perimeter when there was a shout from the Brigade Major: 'There's more of them coming through the pass!'

Seven

Fat, squat, ugly – a toad upon a throne, but an immensely powerful one: Rajah Mohan Singh's neck overhung a golden collar-band in rolls of heavy flesh, and his eyes, small and close-set, jet black, stared at the supposed Afghan as though in transmission of his power via the messenger to the recalcitrant Amir in Kabul.

'Your name?' he asked.

'Amanuallh Sarabi, Highness.'

'And you come from Kabul with evil

tidings?'

'That is so, Highness.'

'Why has your Amir changed his mind?'

Ogilvie shrugged and said, as he had said to the opium seller, 'I am but the messenger, Highness, and I do not know.'

'Perhaps a spell in my dungeons will bring knowledge!'

'The knowledge is not there to be brought, Highness.'

Rajah Mohan Singh frowned and breathed heavily down his nostrils. 'If your Amir will not send me his armies, I shall do without them! I have strength of my own to fight with. Yet much of my plan was dependent upon your Amir and his fighting men. Your Amir has always been a man of his word. Why should I believe you, when so much is at stake? Do you bring written words from Kabul, Amanullah Sarabi?'

'I do not.' Ogilvie had his clincher now, for eventual report to Fettleworth: Mohan Singh's intentions were clear in regard to assistance from Afghanistan and he must mean to attack the Raj. Ogilvie drew himself up. 'I am an Afghan, a Pathan, and I do not lie. To lie would be beneath the honour of a Pathan.' To lie was in fact much further beneath the honour of a British officer, which was one reason why Ogilvie disliked the Political Service, but for now he was committed by order of Bloody Francis Fettleworth. 'The message I bring is to be relied upon, and is the word of my Amir. Tell me what message you wish taken back to Kabul and I shall deliver it.'

Mohan Singh's eyes glittered. He said, 'There will be no message, Amanullah Sarabi. I shall send my own emissaries to Kabul to discover for myself the truth of what you have said. In the meantime you will remain here as my guest ... and if the answer from Kabul fails to bear out your tidings, then you will die. Now you may leave my presence.'

Ogilvie gave a brief bow towards the Rajah and turned away, walking back past the silent women and their watchful eyes. His heart was thumping like a hammer; this was precisely what he had feared if he should enter the palace, the palace from which there would be no escape. The walls were high as he had seen, the guard was vigilant. But for a while he would be properly treated, in case his mission should be genuine and the Amir incensed by discourtesy towards his emissary: even if Mohan Singh could move against the Raj without the

116

Amir's assistance, he would not deliberately incur his actual hostility at this stage – that could probably be relied upon. It would take many days for the Rajah's messenger to negotiate the hills and passes across the Frontier and then reach Kabul, as long again for him to return.

There was time yet, and time gave hope. But there was still Brora, who had given no sign of recognition during the audience of His Highness.

An apartment had been provided, and after a sumptuous feast which Ogilvie attended in his capacity as "guest" of the Rajah, a meal at which His Highness over-ate grossly and spoke little other than to Lord Brora who was seated at his left, the privacy of this apartment was much appreciated. It was comfortable and richly furnished: the Rajah was indeed playing safe *vis-à-vis* the Amir – no dungeons for the messenger! Yet although Ogilvie was a guest he was a prisoner as well; the door of his apartment was not locked, certainly, but all his movements had been watched by one of the Rajah's soldiers and he had been firmly steered away from parts of the palace and its grounds when he had walked the courtyard during the daylight hours. One part in particular he had not been permitted to approach within something like a hundred yards: a rear section of the great building, with two small barred windows set into the immensely thick walls.

He had fancied he had seen, briefly, a young girl's face before his guard had turned him away. It could have been the ordinary women's quarters or it could have been the transit prison for the luckless women of the Rajah's evil trade, those who awaited transportation across the frontiers into Persia and beyond.

Ogilvie looked from his window; this gave a view over the city, clustered below the palace walls. From high above, and at night with the moon silvering the dwellings, it looked clean and in its way romantic, lying as it did between the great hills of Afghanistan and Kashmir. But the opium dens would be busy and the Rajah's agents would be spying on the townspeople and there would be much fear of the crash on the door followed by the snouts of the rifles as Mohan Singh maintained his disciplinary grip on anyone who had displeased him by word or action. India was a beautiful land but always a cruel one ... at any rate, where the fiat of the Queen-Empress did not run, where the

Raj was not in direct control to see fair play as between poverty and the overwhelming power of wealth.

As the moon rose high over the palace, Ogilvie turned into the *charpoy* made ready for him. He lay wakeful for a long time, tossing and turning, running things through in his mind again and again, uselessly. He had been brought into a trap, and soon that trap would close finally about him. All that was left was time. He racked his brains for some way of using time to his advantage, and he found none. When sleep came, nightmares came as well. All his thoughts revolved in his brain like some appalling treadmill from which they couldn't escape. Into them all wove the figure of Lord Brora, enigmatic, arrogant, an obvious traitor to the regiment and the Raj, a British officer now standing at the back of Rajah Mohan Singh and his filthy schemes. Ogilvie could not believe for a moment that Brora had failed to recognize him.

Twenty miles to the south of Drosh, the brigade had its back, metaphorically, to the wall. From out of the defile had stormed a mass of native infantry, no doubt the back-up to the earlier cavalry attack. The guns of the mountain artillery left behind at the defile had turned to meet them and had caused a number of casualities, but in no time the gunners had been overwhelmed by the flood of men pouring down upon them, and the guns had fallen silent until they had been brought to bear by the enemy on the camp for so long as their ammunition lasted.

Lord Dornoch and the Regimental Sergeant-Major seemed to be everywhere at once, encouraging the men, leading by their example as from time to time they took up the rifles of those who had fallen and blazed away at the circling cavalry and the infantry waiting their time to come in to the final assault. Encountering Brigadier-General Shaw in the darkness, Dornoch said breathlessly, 'I think we're outnumbered almost three to one. I think there's only one thing we can do now.'

Shaw wiped blood from his forehead. 'What's that, Colonel?'

'Follow General Fettleworth's precept, sir. If the square was good enough for Wellington, it's good enough for us!'

'From square!' The Brigadier-General gave a harsh laugh. 'Instead of continuing to defend the perimeter?'

'The perimeter's gone in a dozen places,

General, and the camp's virtually ceased to exist.' Dornoch waved an arm round what was now a shambles of burning tents and looted commissariat; indeed, the mules had mostly fled into the night, quite beyond the control of the drivers of the attached Supply and Transport column. Others lay, like the horses, with gaping stomachs where the sabres had struck, or heads shattered by the bullets. 'We must from square, sir, or none of us will survive!'

Dornoch's tone was heated, almost a sound of despair in it. Shaw breathed out hard, then gave a reluctant nod.

'All right, Dornoch, we'll try it.' The Brigadier-General turned to his bugler and a moment later the call sounded out across the slaughter. The company commanders and NCOs chivvied the men into square formation; there was some scathing comment from the Jocks as they took up position but they obeyed the order. In double-quick time, as the bullets continued to smash into the camp, the square was formed. With men behind them ready to take their places when they fell, the outward-facing ranks opened fire at the hordes of native soldiers. The attackers went down like ninepins; as the cavalry tried to cut into the solid square their horses were shot from under them and their bodies were peppered as they crashed to the hard ground. Dornoch had been right; the attack looked like being held off. The native force withdrew towards the mouth of the defile to regroup, and this gave the Scots and the Indian Army battalions time to draw breath. MacTrease, in one of the corner positions to the north, wiped sweat from his forehead with his sleeve and spoke to the man on his right, who happened to be Private Campbell.

'A bit more realistic than Salisbury Plain, eh, laddie?'

'Yes, Colour-Sar'nt.'

'Well now, you've already despatched the cavalry officer. When they come back, see what you can do with the infantry bastard – that's if I don't get him first. You've seen the one I mean?'

'I don't think I have, Colour-Sar'nt.'

'The bugger with the big white turban. Bigger turban and gaudier uniform than the rest. More tassels.' MacTrease grinned tightly. 'We're all the same! Bloody Francis, too, has more tassels and gold on–' He broke off. 'They're coming back already. Stand-to, Campbell.'

The horde of men and horses swept

towards the brigade once more, yelling and sounding tinny bugles and trumpets. It was a massive charge that broke like sea-waves against the British square. It parted to each side as the defenders opened, the rifles growing hot to the grasp as the bullets were pumped out. As the charge swept past, numerous bodies were seen to have been added to those already dead or wounded. A ragged cheer rose from the packed men, and they stood by to receive the return charge. When it came it had lost a good deal of its earlier momentum. The good old Duke of Wellington, as MacTrease observed, had known a thing or two about the conduct of a battle. Once again the enemy galloped past to the north, once again they halted just outside the defile. As after that pause they went into yet another charge, the white-turbaned officer was seen clearly, running in the lead of his men and waving a sword about his head.

'Now,' MacTrease said, and took deliberate and careful aim. Campbell did the same. They fired together, but the man kept on coming, running like the wind now and shouting his followers on.

Suddenly, Campbell got to his feet and started forward. MacTrease shouted out savagely. 'Come back, you bloody fool, come back! You've no orders to break square!'

Campbell took no notice. He ran ahead, rifle and bayonet levelled at the native leader. Closing the man, he fired and at the same time lunged forward with his bayonet. The officer went down with a crash, pulling Campbell down with him via the bayonet that was still impaled. Campbell struggled to his feet and twisted the blade in the man's chest, freed it, and began to dash back to rejoin the square. By some miracle he made it, though by now he was in the midst of the charge and was at as much danger from the British bullets as from those of the attackers. Throwing himself into place, he rolled over and resumed his firing position.

MacTrease said, 'The next time you disobey orders, Private Campbell, you'll be on a charge. You will be this time, if the Colonel says so.' His tone altered. 'But if that's the case, then I'll put in a word. Well done, laddie!'

Next morning Ogilvie left his room without hindrance and walked out into the palace grounds. A soldier who had been standing at the head of the staircase followed him out, keeping his distance at about a dozen yards or so. The morning was cool, the air fresh, the sky blue and clear of clouds. There were men moving about on their daily tasks, the Rajah's menials – men of low caste whose bared backs showed the weals of the lash. One of the last strongholds of slavery, was the palace of Drosh ... the Raj was needed here without a doubt! Ogilvie walked on towards a garden, heavy with the scent of flowers brought out by the climbing sun. Behind him came his guard. As he approached the garden, Ogilvie heard a shout.

'Amanullah Sarabi!'

A well remembered voice: Brora's. Ogilvie turned. Brora called out in Pushtu for him to stop, then spoke in a loud voice to the soldier. He had His Highness' authority to speak to the Pathan, and the soldier could leave the guard duty until recalled. The man saluted and marched away, but remained watching as Ogilvie and Brora walked on towards the garden's peace.

'Well, Amanullah Sarabi,' Brora said, this time keeping his voice down.

'Yes, sahib?'

Brora gave a coarse laugh. 'You can drop the play-acting, my dear Ogilvie, I spotted you the moment you walked into the Rajah's presence!'

'I had a feeling you might,' Ogilvie said. 'And the Rajah?'

'No suspicion. You're safe until his man gets back from Kabul. Unless I tell him.' Again Brora laughed. 'In the meantime you'd better tell *me* what you're doing here.'

'Orders from Division, Major.'

'Fettleworth?'

'In person.'

'Ha! What does he want to know?'

Ogilvie shrugged and gave a safe answer to a possible renegade. 'All there is to know about the Rajah's intentions. That's obvious, surely.'

'Yes, yes.' Brora paced on, slowly. 'No doubt you'll be wondering about me – and so will the good Lord Dornoch! Well, I'm sorry, but I can't satisfy anyone's curiosity just yet. If you ask why I can't satisfy yours, I answer that every man has his breaking point and I don't know what yours is.'

'You mean–'

'I mean that when the Rajah's messenger gets back from Kabul, the one thing sure about your future is that you're going to be put under extreme pressure. Torture. The less you know, the better.'

'For you, Major?' Ogilvie asked coolly.

Brora's face suffused. 'For the Raj, damn

126

you, Ogilvie!'

'Then you're on the square?'

For a moment Brora seemed about to strike Ogilvie; then, with an effort, he simmered down. In a controlled voice he said, 'Tell me, Ogilvie: what's been said about me in cantonments?'

Ogilvie hesitated. It would be tactless to say too much, yet Brora must guess that the comment had been far from kind. He had never set any store by popularity, and knew indeed that he had none. When such a man appeared to fall from grace, tongues would be sharp. Ogilvie said, 'Officially, no minds have been made up yet.'

'And unofficially?'

'Your motives are suspect, Major. Your motives for your absence from the regiment–'

'And for being in Drosh? Is this known?'

Ogilvie nodded. 'Yes. That was why the brigade was withdrawn the first time they marched. General Fettleworth–'

'That ass.'

'He'd been informed that you were in Drosh.'

'I see.'

'And Division had been told you'd given a promise to the Rajah that he wouldn't be pursued over his trade in women.'

'I see,' Brora said again. He paced on. 'So it's obvious you're here to spy on me as well as on the bloody Rajah. As I told you, the less you know the better.'

Ogilvie said, 'There's something *you* should know. I saw you in the woman-market, the wife market, in Garwar just recently. You were riding away with a number of women, and with the Rajah's soldiers. That's been reported to Division, too.'

'Has it indeed! By you?'

'By Major Blaise-Willoughby, who was with me.'

Brora was silent for a while. The scent of the flowers wafted, loosened by a light, cool breeze from Himalaya to the north. The two men paced the paths; Brora's arrogance seemed muted now, overlaid by the precariousness of his position vis-à-vis both the Rajah and the Raj itself. He said, 'There's an explanation, Ogilvie. I'm not giving it for reasons already stated – and they're real enough, believe me – but there *is* one. I hope you'll believe that.'

'I want to, Major. A little more information–'

'Damn you, how many more times!'

'Yes, I've taken your point. But I'd do my

damnedest not to talk–'

'You'd die first?' Brora made a sneering sound. 'Oh, it's been done I don't deny! Perhaps you would, but I take leave to doubt it. Those who've done it before – in my view, that was simply because the torturers didn't know their job, didn't know how to keep their victim alive through the worst of it. The Rajah's men know their job very well indeed – damn it, Ogilvie, I've had to watch them in action! It wasn't pretty. Limbs stretched until arms and legs came free of the sockets, and flopped about in the flesh. But the men lived.'

'And talked?'

'Yes. It wasn't always men. There were women and young girls who were revolted by His Highness and refused to bed with him. In their case it was whips, applied in a particularly painful way.'

'Was there a woman in your case, Major?' Ogilvie asked.

Savagely Brora said, 'Yes! Yes, there was a woman. Oh, I'm not saying my hands are lily white, Ogilvie, but I'm no traitor to the Raj, I assure you!'

Ogilvie nodded. He said quietly, 'I think you should trust me now, Major. There may not be too much time left. When I was sent

129

on this mission, the regiment was under orders to march on Drosh with the brigade – or rather, to place themselves in the first instance handy for an attack on the city. If you're found here when the orders for attack come through–'

'Explanations are going to be difficult! Yes, they may. On the other hand, by that time, they may not!' Brora changed the subject before Ogilvie could ask more questions. He said, 'The regiment may be under attack. The bloody Rajah's already sent out a force – I couldn't prevent it, I'm sorry to say. The little bugger's determined to hit out at the Raj and fully believes he can win – with Afghan help, that is. The trouble is, he could be right. If he achieves any initial success, it'll spread fast. Other native rulers may join in.' Brora paused, then added, 'The British and Indian Armies are no more than a drop in the ocean compared with the manpower in the native states, plus those in British India who'd rat the moment they saw their chance. That's what–' He broke off. 'I've said enough, Ogilvie. I must get back to His Highness ... I'll tell him I believe you to be a genuine messenger from the Amir and that he'd better discount any help from that direction. It may give him pause – for the time being, anyhow.'

'It was something like that that Fettle-worth hoped to achieve by sending me in,' Ogilvie said.

Brora blew out a long breath. 'It's a damn pity he did. It hasn't helped and it's queering my pitch. It's the sort of damn stupid thing Fettleworth would do, of course.'

A few minutes later Brora turned on his heel and walked away, calling for the guard, who resumed his semi-distant watch. Ogilvie brooded, and didn't like the conclusions he found himself coming to. If Brora was free to come and go, as he had been when he had made his foray into Garwar, if he was trusted by Mohan Singh as a traitor to the Raj, then surely he could have found some formula for drawing off the Rajah's attack on his own former regiment? Ogilvie had a suspicion he hadn't even tried; to do so might have destroyed some of the Rajah's trust in him – a point that Ogilvie had in fact to concede. But if that was the case, Major Lord Brora was putting his own concerns above the regiment. The question was, why? Ogilvie saw two answers: One, that whatever Brora hoped to achieve by his actions in the palace was, in his eyes anyway, more important than the regiment; or two, that he was in truth a traitor.

Eight

The exchange of fire had been kept up throughout the night; as dawn stole across the sky and brought up the rearing peaks, purple and green and orange, mysterious and beautiful in the cool of the early morning, the attack had drawn off and both sides had for a spell licked their wounds. Bodies were everywhere. The native casualties had been very heavy, but the superiority of numbers still lay with the enemy. In the ranks of the brigade as they crouched in square formation, the casualties had been heavy too. During the lull a conference of the colonels and adjutants was called by Brigadier-General Shaw. The Indian Army units reported a combined count of one hundred and seventy three wounded, ninety-seven dead; Lord Dornoch, his face grey with fatigue and sorrow, reported that the 114th had lost sixty-four killed, with another one hundred and four wounded. This total included two officers killed, three wounded; and seven NCOs killed, including the Colour-Sergeant of D Company.

The Brigadier-General, whose own uniform was bloodied from a number of bullet snicks and a sabre cut that had, not too seriously, gashed an arm, was pessimistic. 'They're set to wear us down,' he said. 'That's almost too obvious to need comment! But they look like succeeding. In which case, we're gaining damn all by being here. I've had half a mind to pull out, but that wouldn't get us anywhere either. A running fight when you're the retreating body isn't my idea of warfare. All we can do is hold on. How's the ammunition lasting?'

The reports were not happy ones: there was a need to conserve the bullets now. Black raised another issue: the Surgeon Major was running short of bandages and disinfectants, and some of the wounded were suffering severely. Many would die if they were not speedily removed to hospital.

'I realize that,' Shaw said, 'but there's nothing to be done about it for now.'

Black coughed. 'A withdrawal under a flag of truce, sir – for the sake of the wounded?' He paused. 'You spoke of retreat, and a running fight. Might not a flag of truce fit the occasion?'

The Brigadier-General pursed his lips. 'I don't like it, but I take your point about the wounded. What do you think, gentlemen?'

With natural reservations, the colonels were in favour. No-one wanted unnecessary casualties to their regiments, and the suffering of the wounded had been plain enough to them all. Shaw was doubtful if the native officers would agree to let them march away to the south, but decided to give it a go. They might permit the wounded to withdraw with an escort. A white rag was found and tied to the end of a bayonet; the Brigadier-General's orderly officer took the rifle and raised it high; he marched out of the square towards the defile, both hands gripping the rifle-butt and his revolver-holster ostentatiously empty. Anxiously, the senior officers watched from Brigade as the young lieutenant went nearer the enemy line, picking his way through the dead and dying, the smell of blood, and the eerie flap of wings from the vultures hovering impatiently overhead.

He was a little more than half way towards the native force when the firing started. He staggered, swayed, and crashed to the ground with the rifle and flag of truce falling across his body. He tried to get up, and the rifles crashed out again, several of them, with good aim. The skull shattered.

An oath, a blasphemous one, came from the Brigadier-General. Black looked horrified, his prominent adam's-apple riding up and down the scrawny throat as he swallowed. He said, 'I didn't expect that, sir. If I had–'

'It was my decision, Captain Black, so don't reproach yourself.' Shaw's voice was hard. 'Very well, gentlemen. Back to your battalions, if you please. The orders of last evening stand: we fight to the last man – but have a care for your ammunition. Your men are not to fire blind, but choose a target every time.'

Dornoch moved away, stepping carefully through the ranks. He was met by the Regimental Sergeant-Major. 'We carry on, Mr Cunningham,' he said.

'I'm glad to hear that, sir. I can't wait to get at them again, sir!' There was fury in the RSM's voice. 'To shoot at a flag of truce, sir, that's the damnedest thing I ever saw!'

'Agreed.' Lord Dornoch put a hand on Cunningham's shoulder and used the name by which he was unofficially known throughout the regiment. 'Bosom, we may not come through this – indeed, if we obey our orders, we'll not – unless reinforcements come in time. You've been a tower of strength to the regiment for many years. I'm not unmindful of that.' There was a lot more he wanted to say but was unable to find the words. He took Cunningham's hand instead and gave it a hard clasp. He went on to pass the orders from Brigade: 'Watch the ammunition, Mr Cunningham. We hold our fire–'

He swung round as an NCO shouted a warning; the native attack was coming in again, the horses galloping at full stretch towards the British square. Fire was held until the natives were almost upon them, so close that in three cases the horses came down with flailing hooves on the front rank of the square. Once again the casualities were heavy but the attack was pressed home as resolutely as ever. Dornoch had an idea the natives had been reinforced again along the defile from Drosh.

In the early hours the Chief of Staff at Division in Nowshera had been awakened by the duty staff officer, who reported a message received on the field telegraph from an engineer company a little to the eastward of

Ford Jamrud, the loftily-placed strongpoint that guarded the entry to the Khyber Pass.

'What is it?' Lakenham asked.

'General Shaw's brigade, sir. It's come under heavy attack from Drosh, soon after camp was made. They're asking for reinforcements.'

Lakenham got out of bed, fast. 'This needs General Fettleworth's authority,' he said. 'We'll go and beard him.' Lakenham pulled on his uniform over his pyjamas and the two officers lost no time in reaching the Divisional Commander's residence. Bloody Francis was sleeping on his verandah, beneath a mosquito net, mouth wide open and snores resounding into the night. He awoke with a start to Lakenham's prodding of his body, a snore bitten off in midstream.

'Good God! What's that? Who is it?'

'Your Chief of Staff, sir.'

'What the devil – damn it all, it's not daylight–'

'No, sir.' Lakenham's voice grew louder. 'Shaw's brigade is in trouble–'

'What sort of trouble?'

Lakenham explained. Bloody Francis was irritable. 'Oh, God damn! Shaw had *explicit* orders not to attack – he was to avoid a confrontation of–'

137

'He did not attack, sir. He was attacked.'

'Oh.'

'And it seems the brigade's being badly cut up.'

'And now he wants reinforcements, I suppose?'

'Yes, sir. The matter's urgent.'

Bloody Francis put a foot out of his *charpoy* and dragged the mosquito net aside a little way. 'I'm against sending more units, Lakenham, much against it. I don't wish to exacerbate anything, don't you know. We still don't know the situation inside Drosh. I sent that young feller whatsis-name—'

'Captain Ogilvie, sir.'

'Yes, that's right.' The Divisional Commander lifted a hand and scratched his scalp beneath the thinning white hair. 'I intend to await his report, you see.'

'It may take weeks, sir. In the meantime ... do you wish to lose a whole brigade of infantry, General, for it seems only too likely you will!'

General Fettleworth clicked his tongue, then made a hissing noise through his teeth. 'What a damn nuisance everything is! Surely it's realized I need my sleep as much as anybody else?' He brooded, scratching his head again. 'I'm short of men, you know. No damn cavalry to spare at all events and they're the fastest if there's really all this blasted urgency. If I haven't any men, how the devil can I be expected to do anything about it, hey, tell me that, my dear fellow!'

Lakenham controlled his temper; Bloody Francis was right enough about cavalry – the Bengal Lancers, the Guides and Probyn's Horse had been withdrawn some while before to Murree to take part in manoeuvres, and the few squadrons of other units left behind were all out on extended Frontier patrols and thus beyond recall until their duty period finished. Lakenham said, 'We must reinforce with infantry, sir–'

'Too slow if all you say is right. Why, Shaw's well north of here, a devil of a way–'

'Mardan, then.'

Fettleworth blinked in the light of the guard lantern. 'Mardan? What about Mardan, may I ask?'

Lakenham breathed hard. 'Orders to the garrison commander, sir. Mardan's to the east of the brigade – and considerably closer to it than we are. If a battalion's sent out from Mardan at forced-march pace, they may yet be in time. Have I your permission to telegraph orders to Mardan?'

'Oh, yes, yes, Lakenham, do! I don't know

why you didn't say all that in the first place.' General Fettleworth settled himself back into bed and drew his mosquito net around him with an irritable jerk.

Not long after his talk with Brora, Ogilvie watched a delivery of women being brought into the palace courtyard through the great gateway leading down into the town. They were on foot, not laid across the pommels of the horse as he had seen those other women removed from Garwar by Brora's troop. They were linked together with rope, like a chain gang; they mostly shambled along, eyes downcast, though one or two more robust spirits looked challengingly at the men who were around, staring with bold eyes filled with hate and hostility. The roped line was led by armed guards to the foot of the marble steps rising to the grand entrance to the palace; and here the women were halted, and turned to face the steps. Watching from a distance, Ogilvie saw a number of liveried men descending the steps and halting until each step held two men, each with a scimitar in his hand. It was similar to a guard of honour at a military wedding, but on this occasion was being provided as a guard for His Highness Rajah Mohan

Singh. The toadlike man, when all was ready for him, appeared at the head of the steps, paused for a moment for an overall look at the women, and then slowly came down towards the waiting line.

It was to be an inspection.

The Rajah took his time over it; going close to each girl in turn, he smiled revoltingly and clutched at limbs, feeling the firmness of young flesh – arms, legs, thighs. It was quite a performance and one that the Rajah clearly much enjoyed. When he had closely inspected all of them, he turned and retreated from the line, paused again and swung round, eyes scewed up as if in deep pondering, then pointed to one girl, and another, and another. These three girls were unroped from the line and herded like cattle up the steps into the palace by a native carrying a coiled leather whip. Ogilvie believed that all three were crying; the predilections of the Rajah were most probably known far and wide, and the chances of the eventual trip westwards towards Persia could be preferable to intimate contact with His Highness.

Ogilvie's thoughts were interrupted: the Rajah was beckoning to him, and calling his name. He went forward and stood towering in his ragged garments above the small, fat Rajah. 'You wish to speak to me, Highness?'

'I wish to ask you if you are comfortable, Amanullah Sarabi.'

'I am comfortable, Highness.'

The pig-like eyes glittered. 'But perhaps bored? I would not wish it to be said to my friend the Amir in Kabul that I allowed boredom to afflict his messenger, for I am a hospitable man.'

'I am not bored, Highness. The views are magnificent, as is your great palace.'

Mohan Singh grinned. 'Men cannot live by views alone. This afternoon I go to hunt the bear. You shall accompany my entourage, and perhaps display to me your Pathan skills in picking up spoor.' He turned away and followed in the wake of the three chosen women while the remainder, still roped, were led away to other regions.

'They'll not take much more of this, Dornoch,' Brigadier-General Shaw, weak now from loss of blood, tried to stand up but dropped back again, gasping with pain. 'The casualities ... my God, the casualties!'

'There's fight in us yet, General. Never say die!'

Shaw gave a thin smile; he was seeing not

only the casualties but the virtual end of his own career supposing he should come through. One couldn't lose a whole brigade and expect to be employed in an active capacity again: the men would have lost their confidence, and any campaign would be doomed before it fired a shot. Such was the lot of any commander, of course; if the luck of the day went against him, that was that and no earthly use bemoaning the facts. Shaw was tempted now to surrender and thus save what lives he could, but the fate of the earlier flag of truce militated against such a course. Also, no reliance could be placed on the mercy of the sin-dyed Rajah of Drosh: very likely all the survivors would finish up spitted on the bayonets, or facing a lingering death in the palace dungeons.

Meanwhile, the fighting continued in its spasmodic fashion: as each wave of the cavalry and the follow-up onslaught of the infantry passed by, turned to charge again and then swept on to gather fresh strength at the defile's mouth, there was the brief lull before they came back in again. In temporary peace the Surgeon Major and his orderlies moved about tending wounds as best they could; though now they were down to torn shirts and handkerchiefs as makeshift bandages, and there was nothing left with which to cleanse gaping flesh sliced by the sabres and bayonets or torn by the smashing impact of the bullets. Everywhere the dead lay in their crumpled, pathetic heaps, wearing either the kilt or the pantaloons of the gallant native infantry of the Indian Army. By now the shortage of ammunition had become acute, and the British return fire was of necessity light. Cunningham, moving amongst the men, knew very well that his Scots would fight on even if it meant bare fists. Sweating ferociously in the strong sun, which was bringing up the stench of death to excite the hovering vultures as they waited with drooling beaks for the end of the battle, Cunningham's eye lit upon Private Campbell who was, incredibly, using a pull-through on his rifle, cleaning it as though he was still in Wellington Barracks and waiting to go out on Queen's Guard. Cunningham shook his head in sheer wonder and reflected that it was terrible luck for the lad: two years hard with the Coldstream to advance his ambitions, and now he would likely be dead within the next hour or two...

Suddenly the Regimental Sergeant-Major cocked his head in an attitude of listening. He was imagining things now; he must be.

But he was convinced that there was a stir in the air, a faint, very faint sound, distant yet. He called for silence around him, and men began to listen as he was doing.

Yes, he was almost sure now. He pushed his way through the massed men and the wounded and the dead and reached Lord Dornoch's side. He slammed to the salute.

'Sir!'

'Yes, Sar'nt-Major?'

'From the east, sir, the sound of the fifes and drums.'

'Good God!' Dornoch brought up his field-glasses and looked to the east; by now the sounds were undoubted. They began to be heard all through the square, and men stood upright where they were able, waved their helmets, and cheered to the echo as they heard the warming sounds of relief. Lord Dornoch made his sighting report to the Brigadier-General: the fifes and drums were moving into view from out of the cover of a spit of rock.

'Relief force,' he said in a clipped voice, a voice that was only just under control. He stared through his glasses still.

'Who are they?' Shaw asked.

'A moment, sir, if you please.' Dornoch studied the marching men as they came closer and began to deploy for action. Then he said, 'I have their badges now, sir. The 41st and 69th ... the Welch Regiment, from Mardan, and guns ... two batteries of horse gunners, the heavy stuff.' He brought his glasses down and turned to face the Brigadier-General. 'I think it'll all be over now.'

Nine

The air seemed to split asunder as the horse batteries opened: the shells exploded right in the mouth of the defile, sending up shattered rock and earth. There were massive explosions. Smoke drifted; when it had cleared the guns taken by the Rajah's men were seen to have been blown up. Broken bodies lay everywhere, lifted and slammed against the rocky sides of the pass, or cut to pieces by the flying metal. The remainder of the native force turned and ran, fleeing for their lives as the order came for the British infantry to move in at the double.

In the wake of the artillery fire, the Welch Regiment advanced full tilt behind their shining bayonets, joined now by the weary men of Shaw's brigade. As they ran, the rifles were discharged towards the rearguard of the native infantry, causing more casualties and an even faster retreat. The Brigadier-General decided it was not worth while driving desperately tired men further; little more than harassment could be achieved. He halted the brigade at the entry to the defile and the bugle sounded to break off the pursuit. Colonel Prys-Jones of the Welch Regiment rode up to Brigade and saluted.

'Delighted to see you,' the Brigadier-General said. 'You couldn't have been more opportune! I'm sorry to call you off, but my men are whacked for the time being.'

'What do you propose to do when they're rested, sir?'

The Brigadier-General rubbed at his eyes. 'I've not decided yet, Colonel. What are your own orders from Mardan?'

Prys-Jones said, 'My orders were simply to march to your relief, and then to place myself at your disposal.'

'I see. There's been no word from Division as to General Fettleworth's further wishes in regard to Drosh?'

'None that I know of, sir.'

'In that case, I suppose I must take it he

147

still doesn't want any attack on the bloody Rajah, but frankly I'm not sure the time hasn't come to do just that. All right, Colonel, you may fall your men out and rest them – a forced march from Mardan's no joke. When they're rested, I'd appreciate their help with the burial parties.'

Prys-Jones saluted again and swung his horse round to return to his regiment. He had to pick his way carefully between the dead and wounded. Half an hour later the Welshmen were busy with the Scots, digging out the shallow graves from the hard earth, using entrenching tools as the picquets kept the ravening vultures at bay with the occasional rifle shot. When the graves were dug, the Brigadier-General left the reading of the committal service for the Scots to Lord Dornoch, while the Colonels of the Indian Army units were accorded a similar courtesy in respect of their own dead. When all the graves had been filled in again, the firing parties gave the final tribute while Lord Dornoch stood rigid at the salute, his thoughts in far-off Invermore with the families who would be receiving the War Office telegrams within hours of his report of the action together with the casualty lists when the battalion was once again in touch with Division. When the haunting strains of Last Post died and the bugles fell silent Dornoch turned away towards Brigade. The graves, with the small cairns of stones that would soon be set in place over each, were now of the past, frugal memorials to join the thousands of others all over the sub-continent to men who had died, killed in battle or succumbing to wounds or disease on active service, in order to maintain the Pax Britannica in the name of Queen Victoria, Empress of India.

As he made for Brigade, Dornoch was approached by the Adjutant together with the Regimental Sergeant-Major. Both men saluted; Dornoch returned the salutes with a tired hand. His face looked haggard.

'Colonel, a word if I may.'

'What is it, Andrew?'

'The casualties, Colonel. We've lost a sad number of NCOs and we must consider replacements.'

Dornoch nodded. 'Yes ... promotions in the field. Perhaps you'll let me have a list of suitable names as soon as possible.'

'Already done, Colonel.' Andrew Black brought out a list written in pencil. 'Mr Cunningham's seen to it. I have approved the names he's submitted, in every case except one.'

Without immediate comment, Dornoch ran his eye down the list: promotions from corporal to lance-sergeant, from sergeant to colour-sergeant, plus a number of privates recommended for the single chevron of a lance-corporal, lowest in the chain of command that began to set a man apart from his fellows and make him responsible under his corporal and section sergeant for the work, smartness, discipline and general conduct of a squad of eight men. There were, it seemed, vacancies for seven lance-corporals as a result of the other promotions; and one of the names submitted was that of Private Campbell. Dornoch remarked on this.

'He's not been long with us,' he said. 'I know his history, of course – the Guards, and in for a commission.' He looked at Black. 'Do I take it he's the one you don't agree with Mr Cunningham over?'

'Yes, Colonel.'

'Why?'

'Precisely for the reason you have just pointed to, Colonel. He's not been with us any time at all, and I fear it could be seen as invidious.'

'Possibly. Mr Cunningham?'

'Sir! Private Campbell is a good soldier, sir, and has done well this last day and night. I have first-class reports from his colour-sar'nt, sir.'

'Anything else?'

'The Guards training and discipline is excellent, sir.'

'I know that. And the point raised by Captain Black?'

'It has merit, sir, I'll not deny. Regimental jealousy, a Guardsman before a Jock. But if I may speak my mind, sir–'

'Of course. Go ahead.'

'Thank you, sir.' Cunningham paused. 'To my mind, sir, it would not be right nor fair to hold the Guards against a good man, or his ambitions either come to that. With full respect to Captain Black, sir, of course. Private Campbell's conduct in the field, sir, has been better than many of the Jocks.'

Dornoch smiled. 'And fighting's what we're here for!'

'Aye, sir, it is that.'

Dornoch put a hand on the Adjutant's shoulder. 'I'm going to let him have his stripe, Andrew. I'm not saying you're wrong and we shall have to watch how things go. Lance is a very fragile rank, after all – very temporary if necessary, very acting, very unpaid! I think he must be allowed his chance.'

'Very good, Colonel.' Black gave a stiff salute; he didn't like having his recommendations turned down. Dornoch nodded in dismissal; as Black and the RSM went off, he frowned. Andrew Black was a difficult man and it was to be hoped he would not now pick on Lance-Corporal Campbell in some attempt to justify his own opinion of the man. Shaking his head at his thoughts, Dornoch went on towards Brigade to report his burials finished. By the time the Colonels of the brigaded battalions had come in with similar reports, the Brigadier-General had made up his mind as to his future movements.

'I'm far from disposed to stay here and invite another attack along the defile,' he said. 'I intend to force march upon Drosh and hold the brigade outside the city, sending more mounted runners back to Division, this time to inform General Fettleworth of my intentions. Comments, gentlemen?'

Prys-Jones asked, 'What if we're attacked in our new position, sir? Will it not be the same situation as now, or rather as last night?'

Shaw smiled. 'No, Colonel, not quite – thanks to the horse gunners you've brought with you! If I am attacked, I shall at once open upon the palace. I have a strong feeling that'll give the little bugger pause.'

'And General Fettleworth, sir?'

'General Fettleworth is out of communication and is likely to remain so. The decisions are mine alone.' The Brigadier-General lifted his field glasses and took a long look all around the horizons. 'Report when ready, if you please, and I'll pass the word to march north.'

Thirty minutes later the mounted runners had ridden fast to the rear towards Division at Nowshera and the brigade was once again on the move, marching into the comparative sunlessness of the narrow defile behind the pipes and drums.

That afternoon the Rajah's hunting party set out from the palace in search of bear; Lord Brora was with it, riding alongside the Rajah's elephant atop which, in a gilded *howdah*, his Highness Mohan Singh sat in state with two of his concubines. Ahead and in rear rode his bodyguard, stalwart, swarthy men with fierce eyes, armed like bandits with rifles and bandoliers. Ogilvie had been

153

given a horse, and rode out between a personal guard of two men with a third bringing up the rear: no chances were being taken of the Amir's messenger returning to Afghanistan before his bona fides had been vouched for. The Rajah's hunting retinue was a large one, consisting not only of his guards and *shikaris* but also of a lengthy supply column bearing much food, for it might take a longish time to find the hapless bear and then to impale him upon the bright, sharp lance-points of the hunters. How much actual bear-sticking would be done by His Highness in person was open to question, but if the day's sport should follow the well-established precepts of princely tiger-hunting, then all kills would be credited to the Rajah no matter how wide of the target his own attempts might be: a rifle discharged at any angle whatsoever from the *howdah* was customarily taken as being the one that killed the tiger. Bear-sticking, however, was presumably a somewhat different proposition.

The long procession turned from the palace gates towards the distant Panjkora River, winding its colourful and noisy way through the eastern extremity of the town. Tinny music was being played on flutes and

154

small drums; some of the retinue danced along, and in places minor fighting broke out as the natives jostled one another. The townspeople of Drosh were keeping out of the way, invisible behind their closed doors until the Rajah's party had passed out of sight and sound.

When the town was a couple of miles behind, the presence of the Amir's messenger was demanded: Mohan Singh wished words with him, and Ogilvie was ridden by his escort towards the Rajah's elephant. The Rajah grinned down from the *howdah*, plumes nodding from his turban. 'Soon there will be sport,' he said. 'You will see how excellent my riders are, my cavalry and my *shikaris*.'

'It will be most interesting, Highness.'

'When you return to Kabul, you will impress upon your Amir that my cavalry is good?'

'This I will do, Highness.'

'You will also impress upon him that when I give the word, many thousands of men will rise against the British Raj throughout my territories?'

Ogilvie nodded. 'This also, Highness.'

'Then the Amir will realize that he will be missing his chance of marching his armies across the Afghan border and of taking the fine opportunity I am offering him. He will realize his own short-sightedness.'

'Perhaps, Highness.'

'It would be well that he did so. His aims are as mine. I shall destroy the Raj. This will mean that your Amir no longer has an enemy upon his frontier.'

'Yes, Highness. That is the wish of all Pathans.' Ogilvie paused. 'When is this to be, Highness?'

'When I am ready,' the Rajah answered. 'I will first await word from Kabul.'

After this, there seemed to be a lack of further interest in the Amir's messenger; Mohan Singh turned his attentions to his concubines, and some giggling came from the *howdah*. Ogilvie reflected on the Rajah's words: the word from Kabul was likely enough to be that the Amir had not turned away from his promise and was ready to support the designs of the Rajah of Drosh. If so, the Raj would stand in danger from that moment. Bloody Francis Fettleworth in Nowshera would find his command standing alone between the initial onslaught and the continuance of the Viceroy's rule; he would be the outpost of Empire, and he must be warned in time.

Still riding alongside the elephant, Ogilvie, looking beneath its belly, could see the legs of Brora's horse on its other flank. Brora was still the mystery to be unravelled. Sourly, Ogilvie reflected on Brora's words earlier: a woman had been involved. One of Lord Brora's leching expeditions, most likely, had led him into whatever he was engaged upon. There was always risk attached to bedding with a native woman, but perhaps Brora, who had not come out with the original draft from Invermore, had still not been long enough on Indian service to appreciate them all. On the other hand, he was certainly no innocent abroad...

The procession began soon to approach the west bank of the Panjkora running down from the mountains of the Hindu Kush; by now the sun was moving down the sky; there would not be many hours of daylight left. After such sport as he could find the Rajah would make camp for the night, and in the early hours of next morning would resume the hunt.

Marching north through the passes for Drosh, Shaw's brigade had come under further attack, this time by brigands who had appeared suddenly upon the heights to pick off the advancing picquets, the soldiers who had scaled the lower slopes to gain the high ground and act as a flank guard.

The order was passed by Brigade to take cover, and the men found what shelter they could behind boulders and jagged outcrops of rock. The Brigade Major, making his way towards the Brigadier-General who was crouched with Lord Dornoch in the doubtful cover of a clump of scraggy bushes, was picked off from the heights and fell dead upon the floor of the pass. The Brigadier-General swore savagely as the word reached him. He said, 'We're going to be pinned down, Dornoch, no damn movement possible!'

'We can accept a little delay,' Dornoch responded, 'till they've been despatched.' A bullet from a *jezail* smacked into the ground close by him, and ricocheted away with an angry buzz to expend itself harmlessly against the side of the pass. Dornoch studied the peaks through his field-glasses; as he did so, a head showed and a *jezail* came up. The Pathan had no time to take aim: he had been spotted from the pass in the instant that he showed, and Dornoch watched the body jerk upright as a bullet took it. It lurched forward and fell, spread-eagled, bouncing off the rock, twisting and turning in its rapid descent, then crashed to be pulped on the floor of the pass.

The Brigadier-General watched, his face grim. 'One gone,' he said. 'A question of time ... and a little delay *is* acceptable, perhaps. With reservations, that is!' He laughed.

Dornoch lifted an eyebrow. 'Reservations, General?'

'Yes. Bloody Francis! It could give him time to overtake us with a mounted runner.'

'And he could countermand your intentions?'

Shaw nodded. 'Fettleworth always plays safe, does he not?'

'True. But it's an ill wind, General. You're taking a risk, if I may say so without offence. If Division countermands in time, you'll be off that particular hook!'

'I'm not too worried about hooks, Dornoch,' Shaw said briefly. He offered no further comment; the exchange of fire proceeded. As ever in similar circumstances, the advantage lay with the Pathans in their lofty positions; they were picking off men here and there whilst remaining largely unscathed themselves. So far it had not been possible to make a reliable estimate of the numbers of Pathans engaged, but Dornoch

159

believed them to be no more than around a dozen strong. Not for the first time, he pondered on the actual impact of such random attacks on British troops; no small force of Pathans could remotely expect to overcome a brigade, so why bother? The answer lay in two things: the first was the innate determination of the Pathan to kill anyone he saw as his enemy or who tried to impose any kind of law and order on a lawless terrain; the second was more sinister and Dornoch remarked on it to the Brigadier-General.

'A pinning-down with intent, do you suppose, sir?'

'To hold us till the damn Rajah can send in another full attack? I've had that in mind, I admit. Nothing we can do about it, if that's the case.'

'We're as well placed to fight it off here as anywhere else in the pass, I suppose.'

'I wanted to get through to wider ground first.' Shaw brought out his watch: half an hour had passed, and no sign of the attack being withdrawn. He pulled at his chin, frowning. If he ordered the troops to march on, there would be many casualties; on the other hand, movement would bring the Pathans out into the open, when they could be the more quickly picked off – but that depended on how many there were. Shaw's view now was that the Pathans probably numbered a couple of dozen. He said, 'We may have to wait for darkness, Dornoch. A confounded nuisance but it can't be helped. Any suggestions?'

'We could detach some men to the rear, sir, with orders to climb out of the pass behind the Pathans, and outflank them.'

'Tricky. Any such movement would be spotted instantly.'

'We might get away with it.' Dornoch hesitated. 'In my view it's worth a try. My Scots are experienced enough at this sort of thing.'

'I know, but I dislike sending good men to what I regard as certain death. We've lost enough already, God knows!' Shaw lifted his glasses again to scan the heights. After some moments, he said, 'We'll stay as we are for the time being, Dornoch, but we'll have an outflanking party up our sleeve in case we need it. See to a detail, if you please.'

'Very good, sir.' Dornoch cupped his hands round his mouth and called down the pass as the bullets kicked up the dust. 'Captain Black!'

There was no answer; Dornoch turned to

his runner. 'I'm sorry, MacArthur, but I need the Adjutant. Try to find him – and watch out for yourself.'

'Aye, sir.' Private MacArthur squirmed away on his stomach, keeping in such cover as he was able to find on the move. He didn't appear to have been seen; there was no noticeable increase in the rate of fire from the *jezails*, and soon he had vanished from the Colonel's view. Shaw and Dornoch waited; after what seemed an age movement was seen along the track and MacArthur and Black came into focus, both keeping close to the ground. As they came nearer, there was a sharp cry and MacArthur half rose, his back arched, his face contorted. Without thinking Lord Dornoch got to his feet and ran towards the soldier, bent low. Reaching him in safety, he took him in his arms and laid him gently on the ground; he was about to shout for a medical orderly and a *doolie-wallah* with a stretcher when he saw it was too late: MacArthur was dead, with a blackened patch on his uniform and a neat hole in his back. The Adjutant was looking white and sick, and once again Lord Dornoch found himself wishing Brora was present, Brora who had no nerves in his body and no fear of anything in his make-up. Andrew Black would be a poor successor if he, the Colonel, should die that day.

Black said, 'You wanted me, Colonel.'

'Yes.' Dornoch gave him a sweeping look. 'Pull yourself together, man! You look like a recruit at his first action!'

'I'm sorry, Colonel. I – I feel unwell.'

'In that case you must contain yourself till we're clear. In the meantime, the Brigadier-General wishes to have men ready for an outflanking movement. I'd be obliged if you'd detail a sergeant and four sections to report for orders at Brigade.' Dornoch pointed. 'That's Brigade – behind the bushes. All right?'

'Yes, Colonel.'

'See to it at once, then.'

Black crawled away, looking out for the Regimental Sergeant-Major or a company commander. Dornoch, keeping in cover as far as possible, made a run for it back to the Brigadier-General and reported. The firing was kept up from both sides; the brigade remained pinned down. Within a quarter of an hour the detail was seen approaching under Sergeant Rennie of B Company, with a corporal and lance-corporal: Dornoch saw that the latter was Campbell, who had now been given his promotion in the field but would be unable to wear his single chevron until the regiment returned to cantonments and material became available. As Sergeant Rennie came forward on his stomach, his water-bottle and field equipment banging over the rocky ground, Dornoch passed brief orders. If and when the word was given by the Brigadier-General, Rennie was to lead his four sections to the rear and when he found a suitable spot to climb he was to split his force in half, and scale the heights on both sides of the pass.

'Come up in the Pathans' rear,' Dornoch said, 'and attack the moment you're close enough.'

'Aye, sir.'

'You'll have supporting fire from the pass. I'll arrange a diversion when the time comes – that should help. I want the Pathans to have the impression that reinforcements are coming in and that they're about to be attacked in strength from the rear. Everything will depend on your getting into position without being seen.'

His Highness Mohan Singh was after the sloth bear, the Aswail, a denizen of India's mountain regions. Ogilvie knew that the sport of pig-sticking had derived from bear-

164

sticking; in more recent years there had been a shortage of bear, but plenty of wild pig, though not in these parts – the terrain was unsuitable for the wild boar, who preferred swampy regions, into the mire of which it was prevented by its broad, spreading feet from sinking. His Highness, it transpired, had declared the sloth bear a protected species, to be allowed to live and breed to be chased and killed by his own *shikaris* alone. Any other man who killed the sloth bear would die himself by His Highness' order. Thus honoured, the grotesque, unwieldy creature, harmless enough if unmolested, slumbered the daylight hours away in its sheltered den; it avoided daylight movement since its feet happened to be highly sensitive to heat, and the soles suffered from the bare rocks and stones superheated by the sun. The usual method of killing was to track the beast to its sleeping quarters and despatch it in its drowsy state.

'Not sporting,' Brora said. He was riding behind the Rajah with Ogilvie, and as in the palace garden earlier, the escort had withdrawn a little way though they remained on the alert and ready for any sudden dash to the rear. 'Damn animal hasn't a chance – not unless the *shikaris* fudge it.'

'What then?'

Brora laughed somewhat sneeringly. 'The sloth reacts badly to being wounded – it grows angry! Very dangerous.'

'It's not a man-eater, is it?'

'God, no – not normally, anyhow! It's been known to eat vertebrate animals when it's pressed, but its normal diet is roots of all sorts, bees'-nests and honey ... grubs, snails, slugs, ants – that sort of thing. Its intake adds up to good flesh for human consumption – His Highness is rather partial to it. Also, he has a trade in bear fat. It's melted down and used largely as a lubricant for gun-locks and so on.'

They rode on. There was a considerable racket from the retinue and Ogilvie wondered it didn't wake every sloth bear in the vicinity. Possibly, even with the Rajah's conversation methods, there were not too many of the bears around ... the mounted *shikaris* with their long lances were poking and prodding all shady spots behind rocks and boulders, being encouraged by the Rajah who was showing signs of much excitement, anticipatory of blood about to be spilled. There was a curious thrill running through the whole gaudy gathering, as though everyone present was attempting to be at one with

His Highness and his pleasures lest something should go wrong and blame be scattered wholesale for an imperfect involvement of mind and spirit and body. It was an unhealthy feeling; and suddenly it became unhealthier when, from ahead of the Rajah, a shout came, to be followed by many others as one of the hunters lunged with his lance and a high, whining sound of pain rose above the noise and chatter from the hunt followers.

Unable to see from behind the advancing elephant's bottom, Ogilvie brought his horse round to the flank. As he did so a large, hairy form rose apparently from the very ground some distance ahead, standing for a moment on its hind paws and swiping around itself with its forepaws. Just as another lance-point made to penetrate the animal's flesh, a claw caught the eye of the *shikari*'s horse. There was a bellow of pain and the horse reared, throwing its rider to the rocky ground. Ogilvie saw the eyeless socket, the long, gaping gash down the cheek, momentarily before the horse bolted. The rider remained on the ground, rolling about in apparent agony. There was general confusion; His Highness was obviously furious, and was shouting in all directions and urging his *mahout* to speed up the elephant's lumbering feet. In the confusion the sloth bear was seen to be beating it in a dead straight line, moving with surprising speed from further wounds and leaving a trail of blood behind it.

The hunters, chivvied by their angry Rajah, gave chase. As the elephant approached the spot where the bear had been flushed out, His Highness' excitement and anger grew. He glared down at the fallen *shikari*, shook his fist and shouted a stream of imprecations; then gave an order to the *mahout*. The elephant halted close to the man on the ground, who was staring up with beseeching eyes and seemed to be gasping for breath. As the Rajah raved on, the *howdah* gave a lurch: His Highness clung to the side as the right fore-foot was lifted. Then the great foot came down on the *shikari*, squashing him to a bloody pulp. The Rajah laughed exultantly and shook his fist again, and the procession moved on behind the running bear and the mounted men with the cruel lances. Ogilvie felt sick; he avoided looking at the mess on the ground as he rode past. As for the sloth bear, it hadn't a chance and never mind its speed; but half the fun now lay in the chase itself and the wearing down of the bear that had had the impertinence to strike back. His Highness yelled orders for the hunters not to use too much speed, but at the same time woe betide them all if they should lose their quarry.

Brora was riding alongside Ogilvie again. He said, 'His Highness is thinking of the brute's feet, sadistic little bugger.'

'Feet?'

Brora nodded. 'It's because of the feet that he doesn't want it despatched too quickly. Those heat-sensitive soles – the rocks are hot. You'll see.'

Ogilvie did see: when the sloth bear was at last overtaken and despatched by the points of the lances – not too quickly – and its head was severed and then its feet. These trophies were lifted high by the *shikaris* and ridden down to the *howdah* for the Rajah's joyful inspection. Ogilvie saw the lacerated feet, scorched and blistered from the bear's hasty flight to seek a haven it never found. There was no more sport that day; camp was made and the carousal started, at any rate for His Highness and the concubines. Brora was invited to join, and did so with gusto. Ogilvie also was invited as a tribute to the Amir in far Kabul, and felt obliged to be present but found no enjoyment in the proceedings as both His Highness and Lord Brora drank themselves into a stupor.

Ten

In the narrow pass south of Drosh Shaw's brigade had remained pinned down as the day darkened: the risk of marching out was still too great. The Brigadier-General, as shadows filled the pass, remarked on the time lost.

'Seven hours, Dornoch. And the casualties mounting. But not so seriously as we'd get if we moved out before full dark.' He paused and once again brought up his field glasses to stare ahead along the boulder-strewn pass, become more lonely and mysterious as the sun, cut off by the heights, left it to its terrible isolation. 'The time's come,' he said as he lowered his glasses, 'for that out-flanking detail. I–' He broke off: there had been a sudden movement, a squirming of a thick body past the nearer rocks. 'Your Sar'nt-Major, Dornoch.'

Dornoch turned his head. Cunningham crawled up. 'What is it, Mr Cunningham?' Dornoch asked.

'Nothing special, sir. I was making my rounds, sir.'

Dornoch gave a low laugh. 'Mr Cunningham, you're unique! Rounds, under fire?'

'With respect, sir, that's when it's most necessary.'

'You're a braver man than I! Since you're here, you're welcome enough to be sure. The Brigadier—'

'*Look out, sir!*' This was a shout, almost in his ear, from the RSM. Dornoch felt himself dragged sideways unceremoniously, then saw that Cunningham was on his feet and moving towards a shadow that had appeared very suddenly and almost unseen behind the Brigadier-General. There was the close discharge of the RSM's revolver and the shadow crashed to the ground. Breathing heavily Cunningham said, 'A Pathan, sir, dropped down the side of the pass. I fear he's got the Brigadier-General, sir.'

Dornoch squirmed forward: it was true. Shaw lay limp, a long, rusty knife sticking out from his chest. Dornoch felt urgently for a pulse, but knew the gesture was a vain one: the knife, he believed, had gone right

171

through the heart. He said in a taut voice, 'Send for the Surgeon Major, if you please, Mr Cunningham – but not a word to say it's the Brigadier-General.'

'Aye, sir.'

'After that, the outflanking party's to act in accordance with previous orders. As senior colonel I am taking over in the room of the Brigadier-General.' Dornoch paused, wiping sweat from his face. 'And a further diversion, Cunningham – something in the van, fifteen minutes after the detail's left. Can you arrange that?'

'Aye, sir. Just leave it to me.'

Cunningham crawled away. Dornoch listened to the sounds until they grew distant and were overlaid by the continuing rifle-fire from the pass and from the heights on both sides. He looked sombrely at the dead man, now his only companion; soon after the Brigade Major had been killed the Brigadier-General's replacement orderly officer had been severely wounded in the neck and had been placed in a *doolie* and transferred to the care of the Surgeon Major, who was in constant peril as he crawled from one casualty to another bearing his bandages and balms. The day was not going well at all; and now the whole responsibility had fallen upon the Colonel of the 114th Highlanders. Dornoch sent up a prayer that he would be equal to it; so many lives would be dependent upon his decisions alone, and he felt this deeply. When Surgeon Major Corton arrived, looking dishevelled and blood-stained, he confirmed that the Brigadier-General was dead.

'A sad business, Colonel.'

'Yes.' Dornoch rubbed at tired eyes. 'I don't want it to be known yet. The men—'

'They'll need to know soon. And they'll have every confidence in you, Colonel.'

Dornoch smiled. 'I can but hope so! The order stands, however. I don't want the heart taken out of the brigade just at this moment, do you understand, Doctor?'

Corton nodded. 'I understand all right. How are you yourself, Colonel? I—'

'I'm fighting fit, don't worry about me.'

'The strain—'

'We're all suffering that, you as much as any. Off you go, Doctor – and have poor Shaw put in a *doolie* with his face covered.' Dornoch's tone was crisp but his heart was heavy and his thoughts were bleak. The Brigadier-General had been a kindly man, and a very human one when it came to personal contact with the men of his brigade –

173

unusually so for a high-ranking officer. He was going to be much missed, and Dornoch disliked the anonymity of his passing, of the concealed and unspoken-of face ... but that was a useless worry and he shook himself out of it. There was fighting yet to be done, and the extrication of the brigade to be brought about. Within the next few minutes Sergeant Rennie reported and was given his final orders. Dornoch said, 'Good luck, Sar'nt Rennie. Do your best. The whole brigade will be depending on you and your men.'

'I'll not let them down, sir,' Rennie said.

'I'm quite sure you won't. All right, Sar'nt, carry on.'

'Sir!'

Rennie crawled away; Dornoch watched him go, watched the movement as his four sections followed out to the rear, with the corporal at the end of the file and Lance-Corporal Campbell on the flank. Dornoch noted the time and began mentally ticking off the minutes to go before Cunningham's diversion went into action. So far the movement of Rennie's small force had not been seen from the heights; the enemy fire was still confined to the main body in the pass and with luck would remain so, but the diversion would help to keep the Pathans' concentration where Dornoch wanted it. As he waited, he was joined at Brigade by Colonel Prys-Jones of the Welch Regiment, to whom he gave the news of the Brigadier-General's death. This, be said, would be reported to the Colonels of the attached native battalions but, for the time being, to no-one else. Dornoch was about to ask the Welshman if he could provide an officer to act as Brigade Major, preferring not to use Black for this task, when there was a sudden clamour from what had been the van of the advance.

'What the devil's that!' Prys-Jones said.

'My Sar'nt-Major, I fancy.' A grenade had exploded; when it was followed by a second, the stutter of a Maxim gun was heard immediately after, then silence. It was a weird silence, and virtually total; the firing from the heights had stopped, and Dornoch saw, briefly, the emergence of turbans as the bandits lifted their heads to peer along the pass. The shadows were deepening now, and the pass would not be all that visible from the peaks – the Pathans might well fear some other unit coming in and firing as they came. It would give them something to ponder on at all events. And only a few seconds after the firing had died, other rifles were heard from the south: Rennie's troops had got there. As if in instant confirmation, Pathan bodies began hurtling down from the lip of the pass. The rifle-fire from their rear was murderous and was being sustained well. Dornoch got to his feet as the attack was driven home and the firing down into the pass ceased altogether. He looked along the track as men came out from cover, cheering their heads off when they saw Rennie silhouetted on the western heights, waving his Wolseley helmet in the air.

With Colonel Prys-Jones, Lord Dornoch came into the open and walked down the line. Seeing Black, he called to him and the Adjutant doubled forward.

'Captain Black, the brigade will move out at once. Fall the men in, if you please. All the dead and wounded to be brought out with us. We shall bury the dead when we've left the pass. Kindly send a messenger to Colonel Tewkesbury and Colonel Hurst. I'd be obliged if they would report.'

Black saluted and turned about. Dornoch noted that his left arm was in a sling and that the bandages were blood-stained. Within fifteen minutes the dead and wounded had been collected and the brigade was once again on the march, now with the pipes and drums silent. Much time had been lost, but they had not been overtaken by any mounted runners from Division, so the wishes and intentions – or furious reactions – of Bloody Francis Fettleworth remained unknown. Which was another thought to trouble the acting Brigade Commander as he rode along through the increasing darkness of the pass.

The carousal in His Highness' camp went on until the small hours. As a good Muslim, of course, no alcohol passed the lips of the Amir's emissary; but His Highness had no such inhibitions, nor had the members of his entourage – and nor had Brora. The Major drank steadily from golden vessels containing wine; he had a good head for drink and remained steady while the native officers and palace officials lapsed into unconsciousness and took up undignified, sprawling positions among the remains of the feast, which had been a magnificent affair of bear's meat and rice strongly curried, hundreds of small birds eaten from miniature spits like toothpicks, and vast quantities of exotic if largely mushy fruit brought from the palace gardens. Music was played throughout upon flutes; and at one stage towards the end of the meal a piper entered the great tent, wearing the uniform of the Rajah's army and playing tunes of Scotland with considerable expertise. His Highness clapped his hands in delight; as Ogilvie knew, the pipes carried a strong appeal to the princes of native India, even those who had no love for the Raj. A kind of masochism, perhaps ... Ogilvie watched Brora's face: a succession of emotions was crossing it. Surprise, anger, pride verging on a dangerous arrogance as the wine took its effect, inevitable even in a man with a strong head; then caution. Ogilvie was having difficulty in keeping hands and feet still as the highland tunes beat out. He believed, from the Major's face, that His Highness was parading his pipes for the first time in front of Brora; there could be some significance in that, but if there was, he was unable to see it.

The piper marched three times around the squatting diners, then left the great tent to the haunting strains of the Mingulay Boat Song. There was a hush when the tune died away; by now many of the party were in no condition for speech in any case. Ogilvie heard the Rajah's voice, addressing Brora. He spoke in poor English; Brora had little

Urdu, and considered it beneath him to make much effort to learn more.

'Good music?'

'Yes, Highness.'

'Your music.'

'Yes.'

'Well rendered?'

'Excellently rendered, Highness.'

'Good!' His Highness gave a hiccup; the wine was red and good and plentiful. 'I send for the piper to remind you of Scotland.'

'Very good of you,' Brora said shortly.

'You are pleased?'

'Certainly, yes. I appreciate the gesture.' Brora paused. 'I've not seen your piper before, Highness, nor have I heard him practising. For a piper who doesn't practise, he's very good indeed.'

The Rajah smiled. 'There will have been much practise when serving with the Raj. He was a *sepoy* with a regiment of the Indian Army, one that had the bagpipes. Now he has joined my army. He is not the first, and will not be the last.'

The feasting and drinking went on. There would be sore heads in the morning, such that might give the *shikaris'* quarry its chance of escape. Ogilvie, who had remained mostly morose and monosyllabic in case

179

too much talking should lead him into danger, yawned. He was tired, needing sleep. He looked around at his companions who were nodding off where they sat upon the silk cushions; they had been as morose as he once he had as it were established that he was no talker: the Hindus mostly stood in fear and dislike of the wild Pathans, the men from beyond the Frontier whose ways and religion were so different from their own, and who were warlike and quick-tempered to a man.

Another hour, and His Highness drooped sideways, spilling some wine as he did so, joining the rest in their snoring slumbers. Two concubines moved to his side and caressed his brow, and he murmured drunkenly.

Brora caught Ogilvie's eye and used his Pushtu, as scanty in fact as his Urdu. 'A long night, Amanullah Sarabi,' he said.

'Indeed, sahib.'

'A walk in the fresh air – the tent is stale.' Brora stood up; his stance was firm, but his face was deeply flushed and the eyes were bloodshot. As he took a step the firmness departed and he stumbled a little and swore in English. 'Come with me,' he said. He moved for the tent-flap; Ogilvie followed, feeling he had no option. Outside, Brora spoke arrogantly to the guards; as on the earlier occasions, they kept their distance but moved on behind Brora and Ogilvie as the two walked out into the moonlight. Keeping his voice low Ogilvie said, 'We're taking a risk, aren't we? Three times–'

'No.'

'They know you're British. It's going to rub off on me if we're not careful, Major.'

'It won't.' Brora's voice was slurred. 'They know I'm trusted by the bloody Rajah and they won't take risks that might mean their own deaths. A word from me – I think you understand.'

'They might report suspicious, don't you see?'

'Damn you, they won't! I need a word with you ... Amanullah Sarabi. So far as the damn guards are concerned, I'm on the Rajah's business, pumping you for information about your Amir and his preparedness and so on.' The fresh air was having its effect on Brora now; his speech was slurring more and his walk was distinctly unsteady: he clutched at Ogilvie's arm for support and wine-filled breath blew across. 'Let's sit here.' He half lurched down onto a wide, smooth boulder well clear of the tents and bivouacs. Ogilvie joined him; the guards remained at a distance and appeared unworried. Brora said, 'I've been thinking. It's time you got out.' He added, 'On your own.'

Ogilvie laughed. 'I'd like nothing better, but it's too soon yet.'

'Why, may I ask?'

'I've not enough to report to Fettleworth.'

'Balls. You can tell him Mohan Singh's ready to go as soon as the Amir–' Brora broke off. 'What you mean is, you don't know enough about *me*, isn't that it?'

Ogilvie made no answer.

'Well, isn't it?' Brora demanded.

Ogilvie said, 'I was to report on what I found in the palace. State of readiness, plans, strength of men and guns available–'

'And me. Don't bother to answer that – I know! I'm not a fool, Ogilvie. And I want you out of here. So you'll go.'

'I repeat, it's too soon.'

'I'm giving you an order, Ogilvie. I'm still your Major and you'd do well to bear that in mind.'

'I have my orders–'

'Well, I'm countermanding them. I'm the senior officer on the spot, damn you.' Brora's tone was truculent but he was managing to keep his voice down. 'In my view there is danger in your continuing to remain in the palace and I'm not having it, and I shall have pleasure in saying so both to the Colonel and to Fettleworth later on, if you disobey my orders now.'

Ogilvie looked across at the Rajah's guards; they were standing easy, talking amongst themselves, and seemed in no way suspicious, but if Brora was allowed to grow more hectoring their attention might well be drawn and the overhearing of a word of English would be fatal. Having this in mind Ogilvie said, 'You're very insistent, Major. If you'll tell me a little more ... then I might see things your way.'

'I think you know enough. There's the danger!'

'But if I should get away, the danger's gone? On the other hand, I suppose...'

'Well?'

'If I tried and failed, the danger's still there.'

'You won't fail,' Brora said.

'But the guards—'

'Let me put it another way, my dear Ogilvie.' Brora's voice was slurring more than ever; he brought a flask from his pocket, unscrewed the top and took a pull. Ogilvie smelled whisky to mix with the wine. Brora wiped the back of a hand across his lips. 'Another way ... if you botch it, you'll be shot down. You'll not be wounded, you'll be killed.'

'I'd doubt it, Major. The Rajah would want to question me. That's why—'

'The Rajah might want that, but he'll not get it, and do you know why?' Brora thrust his face close. 'I'll tell you: it'll be my hand that brings you down, that's why. In the interests of the Raj and the Queen-Empress, Ogilvie! That's God's truth. If you want some more explanation, you can have it, because getting out you are ... one way or the other!'

Ogilvie's mind was in a tumult as he went to his tent and, with the guards on watch outside, tried to find an hour or two of sleep. Brora's unbelievable threat could well have been the drink talking, but he had sounded as if he had meant what he had said and seemed convinced, at any rate when drunk, that it would be looked upon afterwards as no more than his duty. One life – and this was, of course, true – could not be allowed to stand against the interest of the British Raj. And what Major Lord Brora had come out with in support had sent a shiver running along Ogilvie's spine. Brora had attended a levee whilst on leave, not in the Simla hills where he had been supposed to be but in the palace of a minor rajah near the Dargai Heights to which he had gone, as he expressed it, in the hope of good whoring. The mission had been to that point successful: a girl had given him the eye – he had been marked down, as he saw later – and after some preliminary skirmishing in which he had bragged of holding a high position in the military heirarchy of the Raj and of his connections in the India Office in Whitehall, for like this evening he had been more that a little drunk, he had followed the girl to a splendid chamber in the palace where a long night of debauchery had taken place. Drink had flowed freely; and Brora remembered, vaguely, appending his signature to what he had been told was the Hindu equivalent of an English book of remembrances, a mere token by which to cherish a stolen moment. He recalled little else. Come the morning, he had found himself girl-less and inside the palace of Drosh, with many high officials of the Rajah's household looking down at his recovery from drink-inspired unconsciousness. Taken before His Highness Mohan Singh, Brora had been pressed to render a service. If he refused, then a report would be sent to the Lieutenant-General sahib commanding in Nowshera and to His Excellency the Viceroy of India in Calcutta, indicating that Brora was deeply involved in the trade in women both ways across the Frontier; what he had scrawled his signature on the night before had been a receipt for many *lakhs* of rupees as his share of the profit from recent transactions. The service that was now required in order to bring about the suppression of the receipt and the reports was simple: Brora was to sign another document, already drawn up, guaranteeing Rajah Mohan Singh immunity in the name of the Raj from any interference with his trade and any other desires. This guarantee was in duplicate, and a copy would be sent by messenger all the way to Calcutta. Brora had signed it, believing that it would be seen in Calcutta for what it was worth; he was convinced that the Rajah and his officials had in fact believed him to be of higher rank than he was. He had attended the levee in mufti and fancied he had been mistaken for a full General recently arrived from the War Office in Whitehall. It was implicitly believed by the Rajah, who was in many ways a simple man, that the immunity given by the signature of no less a person than the Earl of Brora would last for long enough to enable himself and his ally the Amir in Kabul to amass without interference strong enough forces to march against the Raj. Brora, who had an overwhelming need to get that signed money receipt back in his own hands, had not disabused the Rajah of this belief; Brora wished to remain in the palace until he had settled his scores and untarnished his reputation. In the event it appeared that the Rajah's message had taken longer to reach Calcutta than expected, and in the meantime the Raj had sent troops in – the first arrival of the brigade upon his doorstep had been a great surprise to the Rajah and indeed to Brora. Brora had been unable to prevent the Rajah from mounting his attack, mortified though he had been to know that his own regiment had been involved. Over the succeeding weeks Brora had ingratiated himself with His Highness, making him believe that the availability of women and a great deal of promised cash was becoming a better prospect than returning to the Queen's service; and he was by now accepted as having cut adrift from the Raj. Ogilvie had asked why Brora could not escape with him. Brora repeated that he had scores to settle with Rajah Mohan Singh, among them the recovery of the incriminating receipt.

'And the Raj?' Ogilvie asked.

'The Raj?'

'I understood you to invoke the Raj, Major – when you said you'd make sure I died if–'

'Yes. For my part I shall be attempting to inhibit the bloody Rajah's military capabilities, Ogilvie. If I can do that, then the threat of attack withers. That's to the advantage of the Raj, is it not?'

With reluctance, under pressure, Ogilvie had agreed to make the attempt. The reluctance was not in fact one hundred per cent; he had no desire to remain a moment longer than was necessary and he now seemed to have the complete picture in regard to Brora, whose story he had no reason to doubt. Brora had said that he wanted Division to know the truth; if he was killed before the story reached Dornoch and Fettleworth, then he would be written down as a traitor, which he was not – or not, at any rate, by intent. The escape was to be made during the forthcoming day's sport, when once again any sloth bears would be driven from their resting places in the crevices and caverns. If Ogilvie had any chance at all, he should have it during the excitement of the kill when all eyes would be on the valiant *shikaris*. Except the eyes of his personal escort, and it would be up to him to outwit them and outride them. Brora promised what diversionary help he could offer, always provided it was not seen as such. Ogilvie's heart was in his boots as the Rajah and his followers left the camp during the morning, accompanied again by their tinny bugles and drums and by all the panoply of the chase. Once more the supposed Amanullah Sarabi was bidden to ride alongside the Rajah's elephant, with Brora on its other side. This was not propitious, and Ogilvie's heart sank farther. The day proved an abortive one; not a bear was found and His Highness' temper grew worse and worse as time passed emptily. He wished to see blood. He railed at the *shikaris*, screaming at them that Amanullah Sarabi would take a sorry tale back to Kabul. Ogilvie half expected the unfortunate hunters to be lined up and shot by the Rajah's cavalry. When, in a petulant rage, His Highness ordered the abandonment of the sport, Ogilvie realized that his chances of escape were nil. Brora would be savage by now, regretting the revelations made whilst full of wine and whisky.

The procession was turned towards Drosh: the Rajah was going home. Ogilvie's eye darted this way and that, seeking some way of riding clear and gaining cover. It would have been possible enough had it not been for his personal guard; the terrain lent itself to a fast disappearance that would give real hope of getting away with it, but the escort was much too alert and he would be caught before he had gone a dozen yards.

Nevertheless, the chance came.

It came when the head of the procession had the watchtowers of the palace in sight; it came when there was a yell of terror from one of the *shikaris*, a deep growling sound from close to the Rajah's elephant, and a flash of golden yellow that lifted into the air and hurtled with the speed of light towards the elephant.

Eleven

There was a scream from His Highness as he saw the leopard's sudden leap. He tried, without much success, to cower down in the *howdah*. Everyone shouted at once, and shots were fired wildly, perhaps in an attempt to scare the animal away. If so, they failed to succeed. For a moment the leopard stood poised over the *howdah*, growling deeply, waving its tail; then, as the terrified elephant trumpeted and plunged through the Rajah's hordes of followers, the marauding beast seized the arm of one of the concubines, taking the flesh between its teeth, and jumped down to the ground carrying the woman with it.

Moving with astonishing speed considering its burden, it headed straight for Ogilvie, bumping the screaming woman behind it over the rough ground. Ogilvie's horse reared up, neighing with fright. The leopard checked for a moment, its eyes blazing and its tail waving. A moment later a bullet from one of the *shikaris*, missing the leopard, took Ogilvie's horse between the eyes and it fell headlong, pitching Ogilvie over its head. At once, growling menacingly, the leopard let go the Rajah's concubine and leaped upon Ogilvie just as he scrambled to his feet. A paw caught his shoulder as the brute sprang, and both of them crashed to the ground together. Growling horribly, close to Ogilvie's ear, the leopard shook him as a terrier would shake a rat.

'It's disgraceful! Utterly disgraceful and I won't have it, damned if I will!' Lieutenant-General Francis Fettleworth stormed about his Nowshera headquarters, almost tearing his hair. He had been in a great state ever since the second despatch from Shaw's brigade had been ridden in, bringing tidings that the Brigadier-General was taking his force, now including the Welch Regiment, through the pass to assemble before the city of Drosh. 'The feller must be stark, staring mad – *must* be – all those casualties and he marches on to confront that bloody little Rajah in direct defiance of my orders!'

'The situation may have changed, sir–'

'Oh, balls.'

'But in the Brigade Commander's view, don't you see–'

'Well, he's purblind, then, and I do wish you wouldn't always damn well *argue*, Lakenham, it's not becoming in a Chief of Staff, I've said so before now.'

'But–'

'I'll have him damn well Court Martialled upon his return,' Bloody Francis said vengefully, his protuberant blue eyes gleaming with dislike of his whole command. He continued storming about the room for a little longer, while his Chief of Staff and ADC waited forbearingly for him to simmer down: the tirade, which had grown repetitious by now, had lasted some half-hour already. It ended suddenly and thankfully when the Commander of Her Majesty's First Division thumped angrily into the swivel chair behind his desk. 'Thing is this: it's damn well *done* now, is it not?'

'Yes, sir,' Lakenham said tartly.

'Don't take that tone with me, Chief of Staff.' Bloody Francis pushed angrily at his silver-mounted blotter and the piles of papers awaiting his personal attention. He went on, sounding aggrieved, 'Well, what do we do now?'

Lakenham said, 'There are two courses of

action open to you. One, send orders for the brigade to withdraw–'

'I'm going to.'

'Really, sir?'

'Yes, really, damn you.'

Lakenham coughed. 'Do you think that's wise – on further reflection?'

'Why the devil not, for God's sake?'

Lakenham raised his eyebrows at the curious juxtaposition of appealed-to authorities. He said, 'Consider if you will, sir. Shaw made his decision to advance in the light of his current and local knowledge–'

'How d'you know that? How can you be sure?'

'Simple deduction, sir. Almost a truism.'

'A what?'

'It's unimportant, sir.' Lakenham hurried on before there was a further delay. 'What I'm saying is this: to order the brigade to pull back to what in its commander's view may well be an untenable position could be to order its destruction–'

'Why didn't you say so before, then?'

'I did, sir. Almost half an hour ago.'

'No, you didn't.'

Lakenham blew out a long breath. 'With respect, sir, I think you failed to hear me. But to go on to your second available

option: the brigade should perhaps be reinforced–'

'No troops handy.'

'Mardan could possibly spare another
battalion, sir, plus cavalry–'

'No, they can't. They're stretched too. It's
all the fault of those bloody liberals at home,
aided and abetted by the bloody socialists
who don't give a bugger for the Empire.'

'Rawalpindi, then. Or Murree.'

'Be damned, Lakenham!' Bloody Francis'
white walrus moustache was blown up like a
nose fringe. 'I'm not damn well going cap in
hand to Sir Iain Ogilvie with a request to be
helped out in my responsibilities!'

'We're all part of Northern Army,' Lakenham said mildly. 'We're all in it together, are
we not?'

'No! Yes!' Bloody Francis seethed. 'That's
not the damn *point*, is it? You don't appear to
understand! *I* command the First Division
in Nowshera and Peshawar and I can
manage on my own, thank you very much.'

Lakenham clenched his teeth, hard. 'But if
you have no troops to spare, you can't reinforce–'

'Quite.'

'Whereas I think you should, and as soon
as possible. Drosh may be ready, in a

position to mount not only a full defence but also to mount a full attack on the Raj, and all Shaw has is a badly mauled brigade plus a battalion of the Welch Regiment.'

'Good men, the Welsh.'

'I didn't say they were not, sir. I said there are not enough of them.'

'No, you didn't.'

Lakenham's face grew red above the collar of his tunic, a dangerous mottled red. He was a man accustomed to do his duty whatever the dangers and difficulties; but his General was too much. Disliking argument, Fettleworth was impossible to argue with, impossible even to converse with since he regarded almost all speech as argument. Insensitive to the point of total thickness, he was virtually unassailable, cocooned in his own pomposity; the one thing that could penetrate was Her Majesty the Queen. Lakenham racked his brains for some way of drawing the Queen into the conference, if such it could be called; and he found it, or believed he had.

He said, 'Her Majesty, sir.'

'Well, what about Her Majesty, Lakenham?'

'She would expect you to make representations to Murree.'

'Oh, no, she wouldn't. Her Majesty stands on her own feet and expects her general officers to as well. Look at the way she puts that feller Gladstone in his place, or used to before he went senile. *And* the Prince of Wales.'

Lakenham failed to see the connection, but he had shot his last bolt. Wearily he said, 'In that case, sir, you have a third option, and that is, to do nothing whatsoever.'

Bloody Francis looked up. 'And wait developments?'

'I suppose so.'

'Yes, yes. Masterly inactivity – it very often produces good results. Yes. I like that, Lakenham. I like that. It smacks of *firmness*, of unshakeability.'

On leaving the pass behind them the brigade had buried those who had died in the ambush. Now they and their Welsh reinforcements had sighted the city and the palace, distantly as yet, the towers and walls and buildings lying beneath a splendour of colour as the sun came up the blue sky. It was a romantic enough scene, as Lord Dornoch, riding in the van of the advance, remarked to Colonel Prys-Jones.

'All manner of filth beneath, though,' Prys-

Jones said.

'True! That's India for you. Better not to take too close a look – anyway, when you're within the ambit of the princely states! Far too much wealth and power – it's all gone to their heads generations back and has become compounded with each new accession to the throne.'

Riding on, Prys-Jones said musingly, 'I think sometimes that we Welsh landowners have a certain undesirable kinship with the native princess of India, Dornoch. You Scots as well.'

Dornoch lifted his eyebrows. 'Good gracious, why?'

'Both you and I have a Raj over and above us to guarantee our position, haven't we?' A grin lurked round Prys-Jones' mouth. 'Haven't you ever thought about that?'

'No,' Dornoch said. 'No, I can't say I have. It's a benevolent enough despotism that Her Majesty wields, is it not?'

'Oh yes, indeed – like the Raj. I have this in mind, you see: I own a good deal of land in Glamorgan. Under that land lies coal. It's Welsh coal – good stuff, and worth money. Welsh coal that should belong to the Welsh people. But it doesn't, you see – it belongs to me. I'd not like to be without it ... but there are times when it sits like a lead weight on my conscience. Perhaps it's different in Scotland from that point of view.'

'Our land's poor enough,' Dornoch agreed. 'I feel I'm of some benefit to my crofters and tenants generally—'

'Yes, I know what you mean. You see, I'm the opposite. I think many would say I was a parasite. I'm sure many of the miners would, anyway ... like the Rajah of Drosh!'

Dornoch smiled. 'Well, I'd not bother about it now,' he said cheerfully. 'You've redeemed yourself from your parasitic nature by taking a commission, and facing danger as much as your miners!'

Prys-Jones returned the smile. 'Perhaps. All the same, I know which I'd rather be – a colonel of infantry, or a miner! There's not much choice, really, is there?'

Dornoch nodded absently; Scotland had come back to him sharply, the land that was physically so comparable with these lands along the North-West Frontier of India: the great high hills, the rivers coming down from the Himalayan snows, the keen air when the day's full heat had either not yet come or had passed towards night. Scotland was deep in his consciousness, seemed to flow in his veins, and he loved his ancestral lands as much as he loved his wife and children. So many years now since he had seen the highlands, since he had ridden or driven in the pony-trap to places such as Inveraray, seat of the Dukes of Argyll by the clear, deep-blue waters of Loch Fyne, or along by Loch Tay from Killin and the burial ground of the Clan MacNab towards Taymouth Castle and the little highland town of Aberfeldy nestling beneath the mountains beside the rushing, tumbling Tay waters that ran on to Perth and Dundee; or along the wild road that ran across Rannoch Moor through the pass of Glencoe, round Loch Leven to Fort William, then by way of Glen Spean and Loch Laggan towards the Monadliath Mountains, the recruiting area of the Royal Strathspey...

With an effort, Dornoch shook his visions of Scotland back across the oceans: one day, if God was willing, he would see it all again. For now, there were other matters to attend to. He gestured to the acting Brigade Major appointed from the Welch Regiment. 'Breakfast, I think. Fall out the column, if you please, Major Calland.'

'Sir!' Calland saluted and swung his horse down the marching column. A moment later the bugle sounded from the van and the men broke ranks, dropping to the ground and lighting pipes, easing sore feet and relaxing from the weight of the field equipment. Pipe smoke drifted, blue in the sparkling air of early morning; the field kitchens were set up and soon, as the watchful picquets kept guard, cooking smells arose to whet appetites that in all truth needed no whetting: the men were ravenous.

Down the resting line marched Mr Cunningham, his cane tucked beneath his left arm, his back straight as a die, his Wolseley helmet at precisely the correct angle, his eye very busy. He halted in front of B Company. 'Colour-Sar'nt MacTrease!' he called.

MacTrease swung round and came to rigid attention.

'Sir!'

'There was no order passed to remove boots. Boots are never to be removed during rest periods, only at night, am I right?'

'Yes, sir.'

Cunningham's cane came from beneath his arm to be levelled at a private at the far end of the company's front, a bootless man so far blissfully unaware that he was the object of adverse comment. 'That man, Colour. Kindly speak to the section sergeant.'

'Sir!'

Cunningham moved on. Behind him as he went, the routine was repeated. Sergeant Rennie snapped to attention before his Colour-Sergeant; Corporal Mackeson was brought to his feet in his turn, and duly passed on the reprimand to Lance-Corporal Campbell, very aware of his new responsibilities. Campbell marched up to the offending private and bawled him out smartly in loud tones. Those tones reached the Regimental Sergeant-Major as he marched down the line. Cunningham smiled to himself and tweaked at an end of his moustache, miraculously waxed and never mind the heat of India or the rigours of a forced march. The Guards were the Guards, of course, and they were smart to a man, but Cunningham, whose own voice was far from wilting, wished they did not find it necessary to scream; and Lance-Corporal Campbell, if one day he earned his commission, would need to lower his voice. Officers never shouted at close quarters, any more than ladies ran.

Reaching the end of the 114th's line, Cunningham met the Sergeant-Major of the Welch Regiment, Mr Perkin.

'Good morning, Sar'nt-Major,' he said

briskly. 'And thank the good God for your men!'

Perkin smiled. 'Are we going to be needed, do you suppose?'

'That depends on His Highness the Rajah. Our original orders from Division were not to force any issues, as I understand.' Cunningham pulled out his watch. 'We shall have some indication, perhaps, in about four hours. That's when we should arrive, assuming an hour's rest for breakfast.'

The Welshman nodded, and looked along the line of peaks leading to Drosh. 'It doesn't look that far, does it?'

'No. Distances are very deceptive in India. We have some way to go yet.' Cunningham took his leave and marched back up the column. Attended by his bearer, he stripped off tunic and shirt and sat back to be shaved with a little water from his water-bottle. Washed, shaved and dressed again, he took his breakfast, a frugal enough one of bacon and fried bread, washed down with strong tea that helped to settle the dust that hung like a pall over the track. He thought about what might lie ahead; the Indian princes were incalculable when they chose to defy the Raj, and the brigade could well be in action again upon arrival if not before.

Currently there was an air of peace and tranquillity over Drosh; it could be the calm before the storm.

Breakfast over, the bugle sounded again from Brigade and the battalions fell in once more. The word was passed for the pipes and drums, which would alternate with the fifes of the Welch Regiment. There was no chance now of the advance being unseen from Drosh, and the soldiers marched the better for their music.

Curiously, Ogilvie was conscious of no pain at all as the leopard shook him and its teeth bit; there was a feeling of having been mesmerized. He was not conscious even of any fear. It was as though he had fallen into a state of total shock; yet it was not quite that. It was like the stupor exhibited by a mouse when snatched up in the jaws of a cat. Although he was aware of all that was happening, there was a kind of dreaminess that interposed itself, as though a merciful God had so arranged nature that the pain of approaching death and its attendant terrors were taken away. There was even a sense of curiosity in which Ogilvie found himself wondering about the manner in which the leopard would eat his body. His reasoning

204

powers remained, however; he was aware enough of a terrible danger from which he should try to escape if he could, but that was as far as it went; he felt that in some odd way his mind had been loosened from its hold upon his nervous system – that in a sense it was 'not at home' to the reception of any impression from his nerve-endings. This did not in fact last for very long: a shot came across, killing the leopard. Ogilvie fell beneath the animal's body. Brora, who had fired the killing shot while the Rajah's retinue all dashed for cover, dismounted and dragged the leopard clear, then helped Ogilvie to a sitting position.

'You have been lucky, Amanullah Sarabi,' he said in Pushtu. 'Luckier than His Highness' woman.' The concubine lay dead, whether from loss of blood and the puncturing of some vital artery, or from sheer terror, was not known yet. 'Are you able to stand, Amanullah Sarabi?'

'I'll try.' Ogilvie was in a dazed state but knew he must pull himself together as fast as possible; his wounds were fairly light considering his experience. The leopard's teeth had penetrated only a little way, doing scarcely more than dent the flesh; the thick Pathan garments had been his salvation. He had lost almost no blood other than from a swipe of a paw that had scarred his shoulder and neck as his garment had been torn aside. He got to his feet, swaying and clutching hold of Brora.

Brora hissed in his ear, speaking English now. 'Too damn late for a break-out, even if you were fit. No good going off at half cock now.' He sounded furious, as though for two pins he would have struck Ogilvie down where he stood. By this time the natives were coming out from cover and streaming towards the Amir's messenger, chattering and gesticulating. Already there was a buzz of flies over the dead concubine and leopard, and low in the sky the grisly vultures were hovering for their meal. Brora thrust Ogilvie away savagely, waiting to see if he fell. He staggered, but remained on his feet, feeling giddy, feeling the reaction. But he made a supreme effort and when one of the *shikaris*, on the Rajah's order, brought up a horse, he managed to pull himself into the saddle, where for a while he lay face down upon the animal's ears. As he dragged himself upright he heard a sound from the far distance, coming, it seemed, from beyond a spur of hills that currently concealed the approaches to the city and palace of

Drosh. At first he could hardly believe it; when it grew louder he had no doubts left.

It was the pipes and drums advancing on the city.

For a brief moment he caught Brora's eye and read the anger and consternation.

Twelve

Some three or four miles from Drosh, Lord Dornoch had passed orders back along the column via his orderly officer, who rode to the rear to make contact with the adjutants of the various battalions. Andrew Black had words with the Regimental Sergeant-Major.

'Orders from Brigade, Mr Cunningham. The Colonel will halt the column on the heights outside the city, but the men will remain standing-to until they're told otherwise.'

'Aye, sir.'

'The Colonel will await a reaction from the city before reaching any decision.'

'Decision as to attack or not, sir?'

Black nodded. 'I take it so, Mr Cunningham, yes. You will kindly impress upon the Colour-Sergeants that the men are to be kept smart and alert and are not to degenerate into a rabble however tired they may be.'

'I shall see to that, of course, sir,' Cunningham said stiffly. Black turned away to pass similar strictures to the Company Commanders; Cunningham, saluting the rigid back of the Adjutant, fumed. Captain Black had an unfortunate way with him, and an unfortunate tongue that irritated all ranks with its tactlessness and overstatement; he was a lesser shadow of Lord Brora ... thinking of Lord Brora, Cunningham's face grew bleaker. Better not to think about the men; he marched along the column, having his words with the Colour-Sergeants as instructed, leaving behind him a good deal of tooth-sucking and adverse, *sotto voce* comment upon the Adjutant. Everyone knew that Black would have put his own embellishments on the Colonel's orders. As more orders came down a little later, bringing the columns from "march at ease" to "march at attention", some talking still continued. Captain Black rode again down the files, calling harshly for silence and bidding the NCOs take names for the next defaulters.

Bayonets were ordered to be fixed on the march and they advanced now behind the pipes and drums of the battalion, with their rifles at the slope, the bayonets gleaming in the hot sunlight, reflecting a moving forest of dancing fire.

In the van the Colonel lifted his field-glasses from time to time, studying the white buildings of the city and the grim palace-fortress that dominated it. 'They're taking our approach calmly,' he observed. 'I see soldiers on the palace battlements and that's about all.' He turned to the Welsh Colonel. 'What d'you make of it, Prys-Jones?'

Prys-Jones had also been using his field-glasses. 'City has a deserted look,' he said. 'Frankly, I don't know what to make of it, other than to suggest it may be a trap.'

Dornoch nodded. 'I tend to agree, but in any case I'll not be falling for it! I shall halt shortly now. If no-one makes contact with us—' He broke off sharply and brought up his field-glasses again, this time upon a bearing to the north-east of the line of advance. 'Natives,' he said. 'A damn great heap of them – d'you see, coming round that spur?'

Prys-Jones said, 'Yes, I've got them. There's an elephant with a *howdah*—'

'The Rajah, very likely.' Dornoch went on

looking. 'A hunting party? It has the look of that to me.' He lowered the glasses and gave a short laugh. 'I don't know if this is a good thing or not.'

'Meaning, Colonel?'

'I mean I don't know if we should attempt a parley ... whether that would cut across anything Fettleworth's trying to achieve. All I'm aware of is that our late Brigadier-General was under orders to remain south of the pass. And I don't especially want a confrontation with the Rajah himself – a *military* confrontation. That's the very thing Division was hoping to avoid, I fancy.'

'But the fact we've come at all–'

'Is against orders. I know! All I intended to do was what poor Shaw intended – to position the brigade close to Drosh so as to–'

'Colonel!' This was the Brigade Major. 'Your pardon, sir. There's men moving out from the palace.'

Dornoch brought up his glasses again. 'You're right, by jove – plenty of 'em, well armed.' He paused. 'And artillery – heavy stuff. I suppose they're coming out to protect the Rajah.' He turned in his saddle and stared down the column behind, then passed crisp orders. 'Sound the Halt,

Brigade Major, if you please. Pass the word that I intend maintaining my present formation until I see which way the wind decides to blow, and later I may deploy into line to right and left of our advance – now we're out on the plateau, we've plenty of room.'

The Brigade Major saluted and swung his horse towards the rear. He had scarcely gone when those in the van, as the notes of the bugle died, heard shouting and rifle-fire coming from the hordes of natives now emerging in more profusion than ever from behind the rock spur, and saw a Pathan riding furiously towards the brigade.

Ogilvie had made the decision to take his chance once the British troops had come into view, distant but closing. He could only hope and pray that once he broke away he could keep going, that he could dodge the native bullets when fire was opened upon him. He believed that the pipes and drums must indicate the presence of the Royal Strathspey, who had been under order to move into the area if not so far to the north. Ogilvie knew of no other Scots regiment likely to be in the vicinity. As the two bodies closed towards each other, Ogilvie was sure: he picked up the tartan of the kilts and the flash of the Royal Strathspey at the dip of the puggaree of the Wolseley helmets.

He looked around: he would have somehow or other to dodge his escort first of all. And there was Brora, an unknown quantity at this juncture. Brora wanted him away, that was certain, and might assist if he could do so without making it obvious to the natives. On the other hand Brora might see the attempt as doomed from the start, and might manage to inhibit it before it became clear what the supposed Amanullah Sarabi was doing; or again he might carry out his threat to bring him down dead. This latter Ogilvie would risk: the night before, Brora had been very much in his cups. Sober, it was surely unbelievable that he would do as he had threatened, and never mind his high-sounding talk about the Raj.

Ahead, the brigade had halted; Ogilvie had heard the bugle and now saw the van stationary, the officers with their field-glasses to their eyes. He looked round; the Rajah was standing precariously in his *howdah*, his expression furious as he witnessed what appeared to be an invasion of his territory. Before long, however, there was tremendous excitement to take the place of fury as the native soldiery was seen to be moving out from the palace to the protection of His Highness and his party. Currently there was a good deal of confusion in the air around the Rajah; orders were being shouted and disregarded, men were milling about, a number of them apparently making themselves scarce as they had done on the sudden approach of the leopard.

It was as good a time as Ogilvie would get. Even his escort looked as though they had other matters on their minds and were arguing volubly amongst themselves. He dug his heels into his horse's sides and belaboured its flanks. It shot ahead like a bullet, like a horse gone wild. Ogilvie just about managed to hang on; it was painful in the extreme but he set his teeth and charged flat out for the British column. He was aware of Brora shouting and riding up in his rear, then the firing started and he felt the wind of bullets, heard them buzz past his ears as he kept his head low over the horse's head. Brora seemed to drop behind; at any rate there was no more shouting from him. Ahead, Ogilvie saw that kilted men were running out towards him and returning the native fire: the Colonel had perhaps ticked over, knowing that Ogilvie had been ordered into Drosh in disguise. A moment later, for

213

the second time that morning, Ogilvie had his horse shot from under him and he took a dive into a prickly bush, only just missed by the flailing hooves of the terrified horse. His head crumped against a rock, and he lost consciousness.

'It's all right, sir. There's a half company keeping the natives off, and we'll have you back with the regiment in no time.'

Ogilvie stared up from the ground, feeling a sickness rise in him. He asked, 'Who are you?'

'Campbell, sir. Lance-Corporal Campbell.'

'Lance-Corporal ... the gentleman ranker?'

Campbell grinned. 'Nice of you to say so, sir!'

'How did you know who I was?'

'Colour-Sar'nt MacTrease, sir. He recognized you. I wouldn't talk any more if I were you, sir. I'm going to carry you out now.' Ogilvie was lifted in strong arms; he drifted back into unconsciousness, but not so deeply as before. From time to time he was aware of the movement as Campbell ran and jumped, dodging the bullets, was aware of the sound of the rifles, of hoof-beats, of much confused shouting. Then the sounds seemed to retreat and the movement eased and he felt himself laid gently on the ground. He opened his eyes to see Surgeon Major Corton squatting by his side and feeling his pulse.

Corton said, 'You've been lucky. How d'you feel, James?'

'Pretty foul.' Ogilvie tried to smile.

'I'm sure you do. You're going to need some antiseptics in those wounds and they'll sting. Otherwise you're not in too bad a shape.' Corton paused. 'That chap Campbell risked his life to bring you out.'

'How is he, Doctor?'

'He's fine, as lucky as you as it happens. Nothing worse than a flesh wound. Now, I want you to take it easy for a while. Understood?'

'The Colonel ... he'll want my report—'

'Yes, he does – as soon as you're fit in my opinion to give it properly. I'm not letting him rush you.'

The Surgeon Major went off. Ogilvie could hear the drums and bugles, the usual tinny sounds of a native army on the march, and the heavy rumble of guns coming closer. If they were to engage Ogilvie doubted if he, personally, was going to be of much use. His legs felt weak, as though they wouldn't bear his weight for long if he stood up – and Corton had left an orderly behind to ensure that he didn't try. He saw the Surgeon Major talking to Dornoch, saw the looks cast in his direction. Dornoch was probably impatient but would respect medical advice. When a man had been unconscious, his mind would not be immediately lucid. When later the doctor came to him again, Ogilvie said he was feeling better; and on the heels of the doctor, the Colonel came up. Dornoch, looking grave and restless, welcomed him back but lost no more time. He said, 'Your report quickly, James.'

'There's little enough, Colonel. I wasn't ready to come back, but there were reasons why I had to.' Ogilvie gave the reasons briefly. 'Mohan Singh's set to attack the Raj, I know that much. Now that I've done a bunk, I imagine he'll realize the truth – that the Amir's still intending to march to his assistance.'

'So we've lost a respite.'

'Yes, Colonel. Unless the Major can talk him round again. I'm sorry ... but I saw no option but to leave when the chance came–'

'Because of Brora?'

Ogilvie nodded. Dornoch, who had been

216

squatting by his side, looked up briefly and motioned Corton and his medical orderly to withdraw out of earshot. When they had moved away he spoke in a low voice to Ogilvie. 'Clean breast, James. The whole thing as you know it. It's vital I have the information now. Don't worry about honour in regard to a brother officer. The Raj is more important. I think you know that.'

'Yes, Colonel.'

'Then act accordingly,' Dornoch said in a grim voice. 'Did Brora utter threats?'

Ogilvie nodded, not speaking.

'I thought as much,' Dornoch said. 'Now let's have the rest.'

Ogilvie told the Colonel all he knew, adding that he believed Brora to be on the level, though frankly, inside himself, he had no real idea what to believe. Dornoch heard him out in silence, then got to his feet. 'Stay there until you're released by the Doctor, James. There's just one thing more, something you should know. I saw the Major through my field-glasses. He was thrown by his horse, but appeared not to be injured. But before he was thrown, he was trying to ride you down and I, personally, saw him fire towards you. I take it that was the nature of the threat – that you were to escape, and if you failed to get away, then he would ... do the rest?'

Again Ogilvie nodded. He said, 'He could not take the risk of my being made to talk, Colonel. I saw his point ... I would have been a risk to his plans the moment the Rajah's messenger returned from Kabul.'

Dornoch nodded, but said nothing more. He turned away, his face hard. Lord Brora was as ever an enigma. Dornoch, as a result of what Ogilvie had told him, was prepared to believe that the Major was in fact acting for the Raj as well as for himself, but acting strictly within his own terms of reference as it were and without regard for anyone else. Up to a point he might be considered a kind of Trojan horse nicely infiltrated into the palace and this might have its uses yet. Meanwhile, as Dornoch now saw, His Highness Mohan Singh was making all speed across the front of the brigade, heading with his entourage towards the safe protection of his advancing army. Dornoch let him go; his brief was certainly not to capture the Rajah, and to do such might have repercussions throughout the sub-continent. But he was to wish, later, that he had exceeded his uncertain orders.

★ ★ ★

'I think, sahib, that you have lied to me.' The Rajah's tone was icy as he addressed Brora. He swept an arm towards the British force, which was still standing-to with bayonets fixed. 'If your words had been true, no British would have come, neither this time nor the time before. To come twice is ill – for you.'

Brora scowled; the advent of the brigade was unfortunate to say the least. All he could find to say was, 'They're not attacking, Highness.'

The Rajah sneered. 'Perhaps they will go away, like the others.'

'Perhaps.'

'And perhaps not.' The voice was like a whiplash. 'If they do not, then it will go hard for you. If I should find that you have deceived me–'

'I was a British officer – this, you know. If I had been deceiving you in any way, it would have been a simple matter for me to have ridden to join the soldiers when first they were seen.'

'You would not have got there,' the Rajah said.

'I would have had as good a chance as Amanullah Sarabi – and he got there,' Brora said maliciously. 'May I ask, Highness, if his flight for the British has altered your plans and assessments in any way?'

'Why do you ask that?'

'Because it may be in your mind that Amanullah Sarabi was not who he said he was.'

'That he is not the Amir's messenger?'

'Just so. But my conversations with him led me to believe that he was genuine–'

'Then why did he run away?'

Brora smiled; it was a cold smile, and as arrogant as ever. 'You have a reputation, Highness. No sane man would remain your prisoner once a way was opened for his escape!'

'Amanullah Sarabi had nothing to fear from me,' the Rajah snapped, 'if he was genuinely the Amir's messenger.'

'I take leave to doubt that. No man welcomes the bringing of bad news, nor the bringer of it. When your messenger returned from Kabul to say the Amir would no longer support you, Highness, then I think you would have taken your revenge on Amanullah Sarabi who brought the news in the first place. And this, I believe, is why Amanullah Sarabi took his chance.'

'To be tortured by the British, to reveal what he has learned in my palace?'

'He has learned nothing, Highness, and the British do not use torture.' Lord Brora, re-equipped by now with a horse, turned his back and rode away, his head in the air. There was never anything to be gained from truckling to natives.

Dornoch had watched the Rajah lead his army back into the city and through the great gateway into the palace. It was anti-climax; Dornoch's wicked and guilty hope had been that the Rajah would attack, thus giving Brigade no choice but to go in and finish off the native force. With his domestic army shattered, the Rajah might well have found his support from his fellow princes, and from the Amir in Kabul, dwindling somewhat rapidly. But it was evidently not to be. 'Pass the word to fall-out and make camp, if you please, Brigade Major,' Dornoch said, then turned to Prys-Jones. 'I've a feeling the Rajah will vanish from our ken until such time as his reinforcements arrive.'

'He'll just lie low?'

Dornoch nodded. 'When he's ready, we may well face much superior forces. We could do with some reinforcements in the meantime.'

'It's a pity we can't attack now – but I see

your dilemma well enough!'

'My dilemma is General Fettleworth,' Dornoch said with a laugh. 'He'd not thank me for stirring up a hornet's-nest before it becomes inevitable and I have to bear that in mind, though a time may come when I'll see a need to cast it out.' Fettleworth, Dornoch reflected, always seemed to prefer to be overtaken by events – or if that was not his preference, then he always dallied until it happened that way. Sometimes he had to have his hand forced, which could be a dangerous proceeding for a battalion commander. But the Raj came first, and he, Dornoch, was the commander on the spot. As camp was made under the shouts of the NCOs and the watchful eyes of the Company Commanders and the Regimental Sergeant-Major, Dornoch paced alone, thoughtfully, brooding on the sun-drenched buildings of the city and the rearing towers of the palace of Drosh. There was much evil there, much threat as well. It was just a question of time now, Dornoch felt. He looked away westward, towards the vast mountain ranges leading into Afghanistan where so many British troops had been engaged over the past years, and had left so many behind. He thought of marches through the rigours of the Khyber Pass, of the revolt at Kabul way back in '41 when the British Resident had been killed and, early the following year, the garrison forced to surrender. Though safe escort into India had been promised, the whole army had either been massacred or had died of hunger and exposure to the blinding snow-storms as they had forlornly retreated. Soon after this, General Pollock had entered Afghanistan with his avenging army, relieved Jelalabad and shattered the citadel of Kabul. In 1879 the British envoy and the whole garrison had been murdered in Kabul, and General Roberts – Fighting Bobs to his men – had been despatched to occupy the city. He had banished the Amir, Yakub Khan, to India; following this had come Roberts' almost legendary march from Kabul to Kandahar to relieve the siege and defeat the Afghans under Eyyub Khan. Since then, there had been peace – the Pax Britannica.

But not for much longer.

Dornoch turned away and walked down his battalion lines, his face troubled. During the afternoon, once luncheon had been taken, the brigade was sent to its tents to catch up on sleep lost during the night march north, while the picquets and sentries kept the watch on their safety. That night, when the sun went down, Lord Dornoch listened to the time-honoured ritual of the Queen's Own Royal Strathspey: Pipe-Major Ross marched smartly through the lines and halted with his pipes on some rising ground to the west of the encampment. Standing solitary against the backdrop of the mountain ranges he lifted his pipes and blew air into the bag, and began to play the regiment to the end of yet another day on service for the Queen. The sad, haunting notes of Flowers o' the Forest stole out over the cool air of night and Dornoch felt a lump rising in his throat. That tune had been heard every night since the regiment had first been raised, had been heard by the fathers and grandfathers and in some cases the great-grandfathers of many of the men who were listening to it tonight; it was just one of the things that welded the regiment into a family.

As the pipes fell silent, Dornoch heard another sound, a sound of foreboding borne along a rising wind. It was coming from the west, distantly, from the Afghan mountains; as the Colonel listened, he heard running footsteps: one of the outlying picquets was doubling back to report. He encountered the Colonel, and halted.

'Well?' Dornoch said. 'You've heard it, too?'

'Aye, sir—'

'Guns on the move. Heavy artillery out of Afghanistan, being drawn by elephants.'

'Aye, sir.' The private hesitated. 'Will I rouse out the guard, sir?'

'No. Go back to your post and report again if anything develops.'

'Very good, sir.'

The private doubled back; for a few moments Dornoch stood in thought. It was unlikely that an attack would be mounted during the night. If this was the van of the Amir's promised army arriving, the first duty for them would be to link up with the Rajah. By morning, the Rajah might be ready. Dornoch sent his messenger to rouse out the Colonels and Adjutants of the brigaded battalions, together with Captain Ogilvie if the latter was fit. While the officers were brought from their tents, Lord Dornoch sent for the Regimental Sergeant-Major of the Royal Strathspey.

'Two mounted runners, Mr Cunningham, to ride for Division. Men with experience. I'll have a message ready for General Fettleworth in a couple of minutes.'

Thirteen

'It seems to me,' Dornoch said to his assembled officers, 'that much depends on what my Major is doing in the palace.' He turned to Ogilvie. 'James, I understood you to say he intended "inhibiting" the Rajah's army?'

'Yes, Colonel.'

'He gave you no idea of what he meant to do – how he meant to bring this about?'

'None, Colonel.'

Dornoch paced up and down, frowning, in the light of a guard lantern held by a junior NCO. 'He'll not find it so easy now! On the other hand, if he succeeds, I suppose he could "inhibit" part of the Amir's army as well.'

'The arrival of the guns,' Black said, 'could precipitate his actions, could it not, Colonel?'

Dornoch nodded. 'Possibly. I think we must wait and see what happens next – indeed, we have no alternative. We shall get good warning from the picquets if there's

226

any movement out from the city, which I don't expect before morning at the earliest. In the meantime, we must all be ready just in case the unexpected happens!' He added that he had sent despatches to Nowshera indicating that the build-up from Kabul appeared to have started and asking for reinforcements to be sent as soon as possible. 'Without reinforcements, we're going to be hard put to it,' he said. 'There's one thing in our favour, however: we're nicely placed for a defence. The Rajah will find it far from easy to attack up the slope to the plateau without very heavy casualties. We just might hold him.'

In Nowshera next morning, Lieutenant-General Fettleworth, not yet in receipt of the despatch from the brigade outside Drosh, was being harried from another direction: a dreadful Civilian, an important man, had arrived by the train from Murree. He had come originally from Calcutta to chivvy the General Officer Commanding, Northern Army; Sir Iain, disliking Civilians as much as Fettleworth, had lost no time in sending him on to Nowshera. Fettleworth was not at all pleased.

'It's all very well, Mr Glyne-Simpson,' he

said in an aggrieved voice, 'but I have a lot on my plate. A lot of territory to patrol and guard. My constant need is for *more men*. And more resources in general.'

'And in particular?' Mr Glyne-Simpson sat back with his knees crossed and hands held in front of his face, fingers interlaced – like a parson, a species disliked by General Fettle-worth as much as were Civilians from Calcutta. 'Can you itemise your various lacks?'

Vaguely, Fettleworth waved a hand and looked cross. 'Oh, you know the sort of thing, I dare say. Ammunition, transport, medical supplies, guns. Men mostly, though.'

Glyne-Simpson nodded, his gaze fixed on Bloody Francis. He said, 'Other military commanders seem to manage. The point is, His Excellency the Viceroy is looking for results. Results against this Rajah of Drosh.'

'Yes. May I ask, *what* results, Mr Glyne-Simpson?'

'Do you need to ask? The Rajah is flouting the Raj, General, largely by this dreadful trade in women. It must be stopped. I understand you are under orders to stop it.' The black-clad Civilian – the black was another parsonic attribute – paused. 'It has not been stopped.'

Fettleworth drummed his fingers on his desk. 'No.'

'His Excellency would like to know why.'

'Really.' Blood filled General Fettleworth's face until he looked like a boiled beetroot. There was much he wished to say: that Civilians were the very devil and ought to be shot; that if His Excellency wished to know why he, Fettleworth, had not stopped the trade in women, then he would do better to come to Nowshera himself and experience all the frustrations of Divisional Commanders in an uncomfortable outpost of Empire; that if His Excellency and his wretched Civilian parasite wished to know why the abominable Rajah of Drosh had not been given his come-uppance, then much more precise orders should have been given by Calcutta in the first instance. But, of course, he didn't say this; or not all of it.

He said, 'I understood I was to proceed with caution.'

'Yes, indeed, most certainly.' Mr Glyne-Simpson was the very embodiment of caution.

'I was not to initiate hostilities.'

'No, no.'

'Without hostilities, one cannot deal with the Rajah of Drosh.'

'H'm.'

'In my view, the bloody little bugger–'

Mr Glyne-Simpson held up an admonitory hand. 'Strong words, General. Not diplomatic.'

'Oh, balls to diplomacy.' Anger had by now got the better of General Fettleworth and was unleashed. 'I cannot do the blasted impossible, Mr Glyne-Simpson, and if His Excellency wishes me to go to war with the Rajah of Drosh, then he'd better bloody well say so. And draft more men to my command at the same time. Personally, given the order – and the men – I would be only too delighted. Caution! If you want my opinion, it's all balls. That's not the way to deal with the blasted natives, never was, never will be. Go and tell *that* to the bl – to His Excellency.'

Mr Glyne-Simpson looked daggers. 'Such a tirade. It was quite uncalled-for, General. In any case, I have not come with new orders from Calcutta, but to inject into you a spirit of urgency in carrying out the existing ones–'

'Which are to use caution, not indulge in hostilities if they are avoidable – in short, not to upset that whoring little potentate in Drosh and never mind that his blasted army has attacked one of my brigades on the march! With the greatest difficulty I have prevented myself from regarding that as an act justifying a full-scale attack on the palace – with the greatest difficulty I assure you!'

'Dear me, I'm relieved to hear that, General! We must accept losses with a cheerful face until the Rajah – er – commits himself. Calcutta would be displeased by any bulls at gates.' As though sensing that Fettleworth might want clarification, Mr Glyne-Simpson added, 'What His Excellency is waiting for is hard evidence that the Amir in Kabul is actually coming to the Rajah's assistance, and that there is a real intent to attack, to secede by force of arms from the Raj. That is one point, General. I trust you take it. The other is this: there has been nothing in His Excellency's orders to prevent your interfering with the Rajah's women trade, perhaps by rescuing any women found in transit by your patrols, and indeed nothing to stop you positioning troops outside Drosh so as to be ready. His Excellency is, of course, aware of the earlier withdrawal and of the reason for it – the apparent presence of Lord Brora in the palace, and his pledging of the name of the Raj–'

'Has any light been thrown on this yet?'

Fettleworth asked.

Glyne-Simpson shook his head. 'Regretfully, no. But a word to the wise.' He looked mysterious and as though instinctively lowered his voice. 'If I were in your shoes, General, I would disregard the antics of Lord Brora and take all steps necessary to prevent the spread of trouble from Drosh. I think you'll understand. I don't wish to be too precise ... and nor does His Excellency.'

Fettleworth's blue-eyed stare rested upon the Civilian; he disliked circumlocution. On the other hand, he had seen something that might redound to his own advantage. He said directly, 'What you're saying is, His Excellency's changed his tack. A pity he didn't inform me earlier. As it happens, however, I am ready. Did I not tell you?'

'I think not.'

'Ah.' Fettleworth had been doing his best to avoid mention of the fact that Brigadier-General Shaw, now dead, had been advancing without orders upon Drosh – such high-handedness on Shaw's part would reflect upon himself as Divisional Commander; he might appear to have lost control of his subordinates. However, a slight distortion of the truth would not now come amiss. 'Well, Mr Glyne-Simpson, for your information I've already taken it upon myself to despatch a brigade to Drosh. It's there now.' Fettleworth blew his moustache upwards. 'Her Majesty's First Division, my dear sir, is *never* caught napping!'

Outside Drosh, more rumbles had been heard from time to time during the dark hours, distantly, as the heavy guns were drawn down through the pass by the gun-elephants of the Amir. The troops had stood-to from the first light of dawn; once the light was up, it had been possible to see the activity: endless hordes of wild-looking men were arriving, pouring down from the mountain regions. The field-glasses from Brigade had picked up many hundreds of mules laden with panniers that no doubt carried small-arms ammunition, and other mules carrying the parts of mountain guns that could be brought up towards the plateau and quickly assembled for use.

Dornoch watched in mounting anxiety. The Welsh Colonel said, 'I'd feel inclined to attack now, Dornoch, before it's too late.'

'It's too late already. It would be pointless now. I *must* have reinforcements. To go in now would be to throw away the whole brigade quite uselessly.'

Prys-Jones nodded. 'Perhaps so. It's damn galling to have to stand around and watch the build-up, though.' He swung his glasses around the horizons; there was nothing moving anywhere except in that western sector where the armies were arriving. The hills lay silent beneath the climbing sun, the sun that would soon grow to blazing proportions and make life very uncomfortable for them all. Dornoch walked up and down, restlessly. He detested the inaction, the need to wait about for someone else to take the initiative. He was much tempted to follow Prys-Jones' suggestion and mount an attack, but knew he was right not to do so. Apart from the unacceptable casualties he would incur, an initial defeat would be bad for the Raj; it could be fatal, in fact. The word would travel like lightning along the Frontier, and the Rajah of Drosh would gain crushing support and send his armies streaming down upon Mardan and Nowshera and Peshawar, upon Rawalpindi and Murree and Abbottabad – all the stations of a sorely-stretched Raj. Dornoch thought of the Thin Red Line ... the 93rd Highlanders at Balaclava forty-three years before. Out here in India it was still a case of the thin red line, although that line was mostly khaki now; a thin line of British troops, thinly spread over the whole of the sub-continent from the North-West Frontier to Ootacamund, from Bombay to Calcutta, with vast distances between when reinforcements were needed. And nothing spread so fast as rebellion...

In his heart Dornoch knew that much of the blame for the British slowness lay with Brora; had it not been for Brora, the initial advance of the brigade, made while James Ogilvie was in London for the Diamond Jubilee, would never have been called off. The build-up against the Rajah of Drosh would have been immense. The doubts about Brora had dissipated the effort, and now it could be too late unless Fettleworth could sense the urgency from last night's despatch, and then act quickly and strongly enough.

Dornoch turned as he heard someone's approach: Ogilvie. Salutes were exchanged and Dornoch asked, 'Well? Fighting fit, James?'

'Yes, Colonel.' Ogilvie hesitated. 'I'm concerned about the Major.'

Dornoch gave a short laugh. 'Indeed. Why, in particular?'

'The arrival of the Amir's force, Colonel.

It'll prove conclusively to the Rajah that I was a fake.'

'So?'

'The Rajah will become suspicious of Lord Brora. He was insisting that he believed me to be genuine.'

Dornoch frowned. 'Yes, he may be in danger. But I fail to see what can be done about him now.' He looked shrewdly at Ogilvie. 'Have you some scheme in mind, James?'

'Yes, Colonel. It may sound crazy, but I believe it has a chance.'

'Well?'

Ogilvie said, 'I've been talking to Lance-Corporal Campbell, Colonel. When he was with the Coldstream, he was chosen for a course at the School of Mining.'

'Yes, I remember that was on his papers. Go on, James.'

'I believe we could tunnel beneath the palace walls after dark, Colonel.'

Dornoch stared. 'My dear James, I take leave to doubt it! You'd have to get there in the first place, and then tunnel in dead silence. But what would be the objective?'

'To take a body of men through, Colonel, and join up with the Major.'

'You have in mind his plan to do some

damage to the Rajah's military capacity?'

'Yes, Colonel.'

'You could be less than welcome! Whatever his plan may be ... don't you feel you could perhaps jeopardize it?'

'No, Colonel.' Ogilvie hesitated. 'With all due respect to the Major–'

'Don't bother about that,' Dornoch broke in crisply. 'Say what you wish, if you please.'

'Very good, Colonel. The Major's something of a bull in a china shop. There's no finesse. I don't really believe he has a plan at all in the normal sense of the word. He'll just charge at someone with a scimitar or whatever he can get hold of. All he'll achieve is his own death and do us no good at all.'

Dornoch was smiling. 'An accurate enough assessment, I think! And now you're going to say that he's a British officer when all's said and done, and moreover one of ours. Am I right?'

'Yes, Colonel. Also, I don't believe he's a traitor.'

'Just a bloody fool who let his carnal appetites get the better of him?'

'At an inopportune moment – yes, Colonel.'

'You're being very magnanimous,' Dornoch said drily; he recalled a number of past disagreements between James Ogilvie and Brora, and the latter's attempts to have Ogilvie brought before a Court Martial on trumped-up charges. 'However, I'd agree it goes against the grain to leave him to it. But the Major's not your only objective, is he?'

'No, Colonel. If I can contact him – he knows his way about the palace, he's trusted, or has been, and he'll know where best to go for the most effect. I have the magazine in mind, Colonel.'

'A blow-up – I see! I don't deny the idea has its attractions. But I can't see how you can possibly bring it off. As I said, you'd never get there in any case.'

Ogilvie said, 'I believe we can, Colonel. If we don't get through, there's nothing lost.'

'You'd better tell me more about it,' Dornoch said.

There was much to be done after Lord Dornoch had given his reluctant approval to what he considered a crazy scheme; as Ogilvie had said, nothing would be lost. Except a handful of men's lives, and such was always part of the military expectancy. The preparations were left to Ogilvie and Lance-Corporal Campbell; first, a party of riders was sent back along the previous line of march, right into the pass where the last attack had come, with orders to strip the bodies of the dead Pathans and bring back their garments. Volunteers were called for and twenty-four men were chosen to accompany Ogilvie and Campbell on the night expedition, which would leave at ten p.m. provided the Rajah didn't attack first. There was gunpowder available in the ammunition wagons, and this, in canvas bags, would provide a makeshift fuse-trail in the absence of a sufficient length of safety fuse. This done, Lance-Corporal Campbell instructed the chosen volunteers in the art of military sapping and mining. His knowledge was certainly rudimentary compared to that of a Royal Engineer, but he believed it would be adequate. The party would take entrenching tools that should be able to excavate a vertical shaft, started as close to the palace wall as possible in order to shorten the time taken to dig out the tunnel itself, and dropped straight down until the footings were passed, when it would be driven horizontally below the wall.

'There's the problem of noise, sir,' Campbell said to Ogilvie, 'especially when we tunnel upwards at the inner end. But there'll be so many troops milling around in the courtyard, I dare say, that we should be unheard.'

'I won't be relying on that,' Ogilvie said. 'I'll arrange a diversionary noise some way off – and that'll take care of the problem of being seen as well, I hope!'

Campbell continued with his lecture, making sure all the tunnelling party thoroughly understood what was required of them; he was patient and lucid, good-humoured and with plenty of quiet confidence. Ogilvie was impressed by him; so was the Colonel when he came along to listen.

When Mr Glyne-Simpson had departed, Bloody Francis sent for his Chief of Staff.

'We must reinforce, Lakenham! Reinforce the brigade outside Drosh.'

'I thought you had no troops to spare, sir.'

Fettleworth stared. 'Oh, rubbish, where there's a will there's a way. There's a Sikh regiment somewhere or other, Mardan I fancy, send that. There's a battalion of the York and Lancasters and another of the Green Howards in cantonments at Peshawar – dig 'em out. Yorkshiremen are first-class fighters, very dogged and determined–'

'Isn't this something of a *volte face*?' Lakenham asked in some surprise, though he could guess that the visit of the Civilian from Calcutta had had more than a little to do with it. 'A short while ago you were quite determined *not* to reinforce!'

Fettleworth shifted about irritably in his chair. 'Matters don't stand still, Chief of Staff. I've received intelligence that the Raj is under bloody threat and you stand there and argue about irrelevancies. I sometimes wonder if you're really up to the job – a Chief of Staff needs a resilient mind, not a constipated one. However. Kindly draft a despatch to Sir Iain in Murree. I shall need more units without delay. I believe he could spare two Irish battalions – the Connaught Rangers and the Dublin Fusiliers. They're usually drunk, but are murderous when roused. All those units I've mentioned are to form an independent brigade and march upon Drosh. I shall also despatch cavalry and guns.'

'Very good, sir,' Lakenham said wearily. 'And their orders?'

'Where's my blasted bearer?'

'I beg your pardon?'

'I said, where's my blasted bearer, for God's sake have you got cloth ears, Lakenham?'

Lakenham's jaw set with a snap. 'Your

bearer's outside the door as usual–'

'Send him in, then. Time for a *chota peg*.'

Lakenham turned for the door and beckoned the bearer, who cringed in and salaamed. Fettleworth demanded whisky-and-soda and the native departed backwards from the Divisional Commander's presence. Lakenham went back to the business in hand. 'I asked, sir, what are the orders to be?'

'Who for?'

'For the reinforcements. After they reach Drosh.'

'Ah, yes, yes. Well, I don't know yet, I'll pass my orders later.'

'May I ask how, sir?'

'Damn it, by field telegraph!'

'Non-existent, sir. The lines were cut as you know, soon after the brigade moved out from Peshawar.'

'Then they can damn well be repaired, can't they?'

'They have been, more than once, and have been cut again. And runners mean delay. I suggest you formulate your orders before the reinforcements march out, sir.'

Fettleworth's face grew scarlet. He thumped the arm of his chair. 'I don't damn well know what they're to be yet! I'll think.' He seemed about to add more when his ADC knocked and entered, looking breathless. 'What do you want, young man?'

'A despatch, sir, brought by mounted runner from the vicinity of Drosh—'

'Let's have it.'

The ADC marched forward and halted smartly. Fettleworth snatched the sealed envelope from his hand, tore it open and read. His face showed shock. He glared up at the Chief of Staff. 'Poor Shaw, he's dead. Killed in action, by God! Another loyal soldier of the Queen, dear me.' He read on, then waved the despatch at Lakenham. 'That feller Dornoch's taken over as Brigade Commander. That Scot ... no damn experience of command at Brigade level! And he's already outside Drosh! With a cut-up brigade! Damn it all, Lakenham, we should have reinforced before now, why the devil didn't you take your head out of the damn sand and offer properly considered advice?'

No outward movement from Drosh had been observed throughout the morning and afternoon, though levies from Afghanistan continued to arrive spasmodically. As the sun went down towards evening and a brilliant sunset, Lord Dornoch summoned his officers to Brigade and informed them in detail of the night manoeuvre to be carried out by Captain Ogilvie. Black, who as Adjutant had been informed at the start, was dubious as he had been all along, and shook his head gloomily. Dornoch, who to a large extent shared his doubts, was determinedly cheerful, having no desire to sap Ogilvie's confidence.

He said, 'We're all going to take part in this, gentlemen. If Captain Ogilvie finds the Rajah's magazine, which I have a full certainty he will, the explosion should pretty well shatter the palace. My original concept was to leave it at that. Ogilvie's party could be presumed to be able to get out again in the general confusion, which will obviously be very considerable. The Rajah could well assume an accident to have occurred since no British uniforms will have been seen, and thus the Raj might not have been blamed. However, in the light of the build-up of men and munitions that we've seen today, and in the total absence of any orders whatsoever from Division, I intend to take matters into my own hands. The Raj is quite clearly under threat. When the explosion takes place, by which time the brigade will be in all respects ready, I shall march to attack the palace. We're comparatively few in numbers but we shall be entering a scene of some disarray to say the least, and I know that every man will do his best and keep firing to the last.' He paused. 'That's all, gentlemen. Carry on, if you please, and see everything ready in your own commands. I'll expect reports by nine p.m. Oh, one thing more. I'd like every man in the brigade to know the facts of what's going to take place tonight. Kindly see to it that your colour-sar'nts are fully informed, and that they inform the men of their companies in turn.'

The officers dismissed. Dornoch remained alone, looking towards the palace; he was restless, impatient now for action, yet at the same time had his nagging doubts as to whether he was right to precipitate the issue. For all he could tell, Brora might have something up his sleeve, something that would settle the Rajah's hash without resort to war, but on the face of things this was unlikely; as Ogilvie had suggested, the Major was not a subtle man and very much preferred rushing about with his broad-sword. Time alone would tell now if the proposed action was right or wrong, and in spite of all his doubts Dornoch basically believed that now was the moment to stop the Rajah in his tracks whether or not

Fettleworth gave him his support afterwards. If no support was forthcoming and the attempt was a failure, it would mean the end of his career in the army; but the Raj came first and this was no time to think in personal terms or to give loding to negative thoughts.

Fourteen

Ogilvie watched as the uniforms were stripped off and the men of the tunnelling party dressed themselves in the stinking Pathan garments, all of them badly blood-stained. Hands, arms, faces and necks were darkened by the generous application of Cherry Blossom boot-polish. No attempt would be made to pass the men off as Pathans at close quarters with the palace defenders, naturally; Ogilvie's hope was simply that the makeshift disguise would enable them to penetrate the city's outskirts unremarked, as perhaps yet another Pathan band of brigands coming to the assistance of the Rajah of Drosh.

Four extra men under a corporal had now been detailed to form the diversionary party; these were under orders to approach the main gate of the palace, which would doubtless be closed against any intrusion. The men would be armed with rifles and grenades, and the grenades were to be lobbed over the gate when the signal came from Ogilvie with the main party; the signal would be given by a single shout of the Royal Strathspey's battle cry, *Craig Elachaidh* – Stand fast, Craigellachie.

'When you've thrown the grenades,' Ogilvie said, 'you'll get out fast – move round the wall to the east and join up with the rest of us.' He put a finger on a rough map he had drawn of the palace courtyard and buildings. 'We'll be in position just there. Inside the perimeter wall at that point there's a garden. The ground will be softer there for tunnelling up once we're past the footings. I estimate the point to be a little under a mile from the palace gateway. All right, Corporal?'

'Aye, sir.'

'You'll have to be nippy, but you'll be under the lee of the wall and away from the moon – and there'll be plenty of confusion around. The tunnelling party will work in

247

relays, as quietly as possible, and as soon as we break surface on the other side, we all go through and form up close to the wall. Then I shall go forward alone towards the main courtyard and try to make contact with the Major.' He added, 'I believe we'll have a fighting chance. There'll be alarm over the grenade attack on the main gate, where the Rajah's troops will with any luck be massed, and the whole place will be full of Pathans – confusion's the word for it all, I think! Any questions?'

'Aye, sir,' MacKendrick said. 'Will there no' be Pathans the other side o' the wall, sir, in the garden you spoke of?'

Ogilvie nodded. 'I shall assume so, but there may not be. The garden seems to be kept as a private place for the Rajah – none of the palace minions were allowed into it at all events. I can't speak for the Pathans from Afghanistan, who may not obey the rules. It's a risk we shall have to take and I'm not too worried, just so long as we can get inside – I'm well used to passing myself off as a Pathan and I'll be first through. Anything else?'

Heads were shaken. Ogilvie said, 'Just one more thing: we won't be entirely on our own. The moment the magazine goes up, by which time we'll be out through the tunnel again if Lance-Corporal Campbell lays his fuse-trail long enough – and he'd better! – the brigade moves in for the kill.'

Earlier that day the reinforcements ordered out by the Divisional Commander had moved from the various cantonments for the long forced march through the passes for Drosh. The Irish regiments from Murree had embarked aboard the troop trains for Nowshera together with the cavalry and their horses. Artillery units, both mountain batteries and heavy field guns, were moving north-west from Mardan. Before the move had taken place, Brigadier-General Lakenham had made further representations to Bloody Francis Fettleworth in regard to the precise orders, and Fettleworth, gnawing at his moustache, had reacted poorly.

'Orders can never be precise, my dear Lakenham. It's not in the nature of orders. Things change, don't you know.'

'A force, sir, cannot leave without orders.'

'Nonsense. They've often done so throughout history. I doubt if whatsisname, Hannibal, had orders down to the last detail of his campaigns!'

Lakenham breathed out heavily. 'I can't

speak for Hannibal, Caesar, Charlemagne or Atilla the Hun, but I can–'

Fettleworth thumped his desk. 'Don't be blasted impertinent, Chief of Staff!' He brought out a large linen handkerchief and wiped his face. 'Sometimes I think you've no conception of the pressures upon a Divisional Commander. To command in the name of Her Majesty is *not* easy – a bed of blasted thorns rather than roses! That little bugger Glyne-Simpson kept on and on about caution and I know very well what *that* means. It means I have to be blasted *careful* not to stir up a hornet's nest even now!'

'I realize that, General, but regiments cannot be despatched to a scene of war–'

'Don't mention that damn word for God's sake!' Fettleworth snapped angrily.

'I apologize. Scene of disagreement, then. They cannot be despatched without orders as to what to do when they get there. It's totally unfair on all concerned and it shows Division up in a shocking bad light.'

'Is that intended to reflect upon myself?' Fettleworth asked, sounding dangerous.

Lakenham shrugged. 'If the cap fits, wear it, my dear sir! Certainly I shall accept no personal responsibility if matters should go awry at Drosh, as well they may if the British force has no orders–'

'All right, all right, all right!' Fettleworth raved, his face reddening fast. 'Since you're so blasted unco-operative, they shall have their blasted orders! They're to place themselves under the acting Brigade Commander whatsisname–'

'Lord Dornoch, sir.'

'Yes, Lord Dornoch. They'll come under his orders – tell 'em that. It's a damn pity I've no Brigadier-General available but there it is.'

'Then they're not in fact to form an independent brigade as you said earlier–'

'No, I didn't. They're to *march* independently and form one large brigade under that Scots Colonel, who I hope can cope. Those are their orders. One thing more, though. I'm about to draft a despatch for Lord Dornoch urging him to caution. Kindly have it delivered by mounted runner to the Colonel of whichever of the reinforcing battalions is nearest, for handing to Dornoch. That's all, Lakenham.'

Lakenham went off looking disparaging: Bloody Francis didn't change, only his scapegoats did. Fettleworth sat on, scarlet-uniformed arms outthrust against his desk, a martial aspect in his eyes as from above the colourful rows of medals they met the imperious look of Her Majesty the Queen-Empress set in her gilt frame upon his wall. She would understand at all events, and balls to Lakenham. Once again the image of the senile Mr Gladstone came to the Divisional Commander: Her Majesty had always dealt Gladstone short shrift – quite right too since he was a blasted liberal not far removed from those dreadful socialists – which proved she knew how blasted tiresome underlings could be. Fettleworth rose to his feet, feeling an enormous surge of loyalty as, beyond the portrait of Her Majesty, he caught sight of his Divisional standard waving from his flagpole. With both objects of veneration in his line of vision he assumed his headgear and saluted.

Then he brought his arm down from the salute and bawled for his bearer. The time for *chota pegs* had once again arrived.

Ten p.m. by the Colonel's watch: Dornoch nodded to Ogilvie. 'All right, James. Off you go, and good luck go with you.'

'Thank you, Colonel.' Ogilvie took the offered hand, felt his own warmly gripped. He turned away, lifting a hand to the NCO

252

of the tunnelling and diversion detail. In their Pathan garments they moved silently away, ghostlike in the darkness, carrying their rifles and a box of grenades, the entrenching tools and the concealed bags of gunpowder. Lord Dornoch watched them go, feeling a mixture of emotions as he did so. Within the next two hours, if all went according to plan, the 114th Highlanders and the rest of the brigade would be in action; the reports had come in, as ordered, at nine p.m. that all the battalions. British and Indian, were in a state of readiness though currently fallen out to await the Brigade Commander's word to move. That all would fight well, Dornoch had no doubt, but the odds were heavily against them and so far no word had come through from Nowshera with orders or promise of reinforcement. Dornoch wondered if his despatches had ever reached Bloody Francis' headquarters at all. There was no way of knowing; runners were always at the mercy of the tribesmen, of the knives and *jezails* and the strangling cords of *thuggee*. One thing was certain now: if James Ogilvie failed in his mission to blow up the magazines, and succeeded only in entering and being caught, then the next two hours, drawing to a close, could seal the fate of the brigade and if, after that, matters went even more astray, they might see the beginning of the end for the British Raj.

It was on a razor's edge.

Dornoch lifted his glasses: already Ogilvie's party was out of sight in the night. Thankfully there was no moon – yet, anyway. That was something to give hope. Dornoch prayed that the cloud cover that had come down over Drosh three hours earlier might stay for long enough. Currently the conditions were admirable for Ogilvie's purpose: even Prys-Jones and the other two Colonels at Brigade could scarcely be seen other than as darker blobs against the hills surrounding the plateau.

Ogilvie halted. His party was not far off the city's eastern outskirts, close now to where the Rajah's hunting expedition had left the day before. He beckoned to his sergeant, who moved to his side.

'Great care now, Sar'nt Wallace.'

'There will be, sir.'

'We'll split the parties now. Corporal Mac-Kendrick to detach for the main gates.' The palace was in full view now; many of the windows were lit by the yellow light from the

tallow lamps, and there seemed to be bon-
fires in the courtyard, casting a red and
flickering glare on men manning the battlements above the palace and on the fire-step
at the top of the walls. The palace was well
defended; and it was possible that even now
more tribesmen were arriving from Afghanistan and also, quite likely, from Mohan
Singh's confederates on his own side of the
Frontier. Ogilvie went on, 'Each party to
split further, Sar'nt – we'll be less conspicu-
ous if we go in singly rather than as a group.'

'Aye, sir.' Sergeant Wallace pulled his
ragged garment closer about his body. 'A
kind of follow-my-leader, sir?'

Ogilvie nodded. 'Yes. Each man to keep
his next ahead in view, but not too close.'

'Very good, sir. I'll pass the word.'

Wallace turned away and spoke to the
Jocks. The details detached as ordered, the
gate diversionary party with the box of
grenades heading west while Ogilvie's
group, splitting into its individual parts,
headed north-westerly for the northern
extremity of the defended walls. They made
their way through the outskirts, moving as
fast as possible without appearing too hurried, past the mean single-storey dwellings
with the occasional yellow light visible from

doorways. Now and again a man or woman was seen in the doorways or in the filthy passages within, people who stared without particular interest at the passing figures in their Pathan dress. The rifles caused no raised eyebrows; very many had been purloined in the past from the armouries of the Raj or from British soldiers killed in the never-ending encounters with bandits from beyond the Khyber Pass. A few natives moved, elderly persons since the ones of fighting age had been brought into the palace, or so Ogilvie assumed, to add to the Rajah's strength. There were not many of these wandering persons; Drosh was an unsafe place under the aegis of Rajah Mohan Singh, and the city's inhabitants preferred to be indoors of nights unless urgent business took them out, the more so, perhaps, when the Rajah was moving as to war.

There was still no moon.

The marauders, as they began to approach the great wall, moved with extra care, making into its lee and keeping close so that the chances of being spotted from the fire-step were lessened. Ogilvie believed that they would not be especially remarked in any case. There was no particular reason, most probably, why Pathans from Afghanistan should not be outside the walls, warbent individual tribesmen who might be thought to have lost their way then entering Drosh from the mountain passes.

Some three or four hundred yards from where he intended to tunnel, Ogilvie halted and waited for the Jocks to close his position. When Sergeant Wallace had come up, Ogilvie passed whispered orders. 'Keep with me, now, Sar'nt – all of you. It's not far now, but I don't want to give the signal to the gate party from where we're going to tunnel. After I've given the call, keep close to the wall and double north behind me. Stop when I stop, and start dropping the first shaft immediately. Understood?'

'Understood, sir.'

'Right. A few moments yet – just to make sure Corporal MacKendrick's given time to get his party into position.'

They waited, all of them tense and expectant. Ogilvie could hear their heavy breathing, but apart from that a full silence was maintained – no rattle of rifles or bayonets, no chink of the entrenching tools, no coughs or sneezes that could have attracted attention. From above, the sounds of the men on the fire-step could be heard now and again as they moved or talked. There was laughter from time to time; there did not appear to be any thought of infiltrators. The watch would no doubt be upon the British force encamped on the high plateau, a watch for any hostile movement towards the city, made in force. A few moments later the moon sailed out from its cloud cover and shone brightly down on the palace. The tunnelling party, as Ogilvie had predicted earlier, remained unseen in the wall's deep shadow. Ogilvie was not too displeased by the moon's advent though he hoped it would go away again once they had penetrated beneath the walls. Currently it was giving good light on the country between the city and the brigade's encampment, such that the attentions of the defenders were attracted even more to that sector, since they could now watch with better effect than before. Woe betide any man who failed to see and report any outward movement from the British!

Ogilvie put a hand on Wallace's shoulder. 'Stand by,' he said.

'Stand by, sir.' Sergeant Wallace tensed. Beside him, Lance-Corporal Campbell ran through in his mind all that had to be done; there was no room for error or hesitancy and he would have to work fast. A moment later

Ogilvie shouted out the Royal Strathspey's battle cry: *'Craig Elachaidh!'*

His voice rang loud; on the heels of it the tunnelling party made a crouching dash along the foot of the wall. As they went the explosions of the grenades were heard from the gateway to the south. Orange light flared and there was immediate panic from the defenders of the palace, a bedlam of shouting and the sound of running feet came from beyond the wall as the Rajah's soldiers scrambled down from the fire-step. Ogilvie counted a dozen explosions and shortly after the last grenade had gone off he heard the approach of the diversion party doubling in from the south.

As Dornoch heard the first of the explosions far below the plateau he nodded at his Brigade Major.

'Brigade to advance,' he said briefly. Major Calland rode fast down the column. The detailed orders had been given already: there were to be no bugles and the pipes and drums would not be used until their advance had been seen by the rebels, which might well be soon enough considering the unkind emergence of the moon. The word to move out was passed verbally by the

Company Commanders to the Colour-Sergeants, who got the column on the move by companies. They advanced at quick-march pace towards a track running down towards the city, Lord Dornoch's intention being to remain in column until they had entered the outskirts when he would make a further assessment of the situation. His hope was that he could throw a cordon round the palace walls, out of likely range of the exploding magazine if Ogilvie's mission should be successful but handy by to close in and mount a siege if the plan should fail, relying on Fettleworth in Nowshera seeing reason and despatching reinforcements urgently. Even if the mounted runners sent earlier had indeed failed to get through, then the very fact of the brigade remaining out of all contact should be enough to alert Division to possible catastrophe – or so Dornoch hoped. His battled-scarred brigade couldn't hope to hold the line for long.

The van of the advance had reached the rough track and were beginning the descent for the city when Prys-Jones gave an exclamation and reined in his horse, putting out a hand to Dornoch as he did so.

'What is it?' Dornoch asked.

'Ahead there. Cavalry coming out, I fancy.'

Dornoch swore. He lifted a hand to halt the advance; the orderly officer rode back along the column, passing the order. Through his field glasses, in the moon's streaming light, Dornoch saw horsemen with bunched infantry behind them, saw them clearly now and saw that they were heading up for the plateau. Making up his mind quickly, the Colonel rose in his stirrups and called for the Brigade Major.

'Deploy the brigade, if you please, Major Calland. We've been seen and you may use the bugles. I want the men spread out on as broad a front as possible, with the mountain batteries to right and left of the line. We'll take the Rajah's army as it moves up the slopes.'

The bugles sounded out, savage in the moonlit night; by Dornoch's order the pipes and drums beat the deploying column to its war station along the plateau's edge while the mountain artillery was manhandled into position on the flanks of the line of shining bayonets. Dornoch's first thought had been that with so many men marching out of the palace Ogilvie should now have a clearer run for his money, though he would no longer be able to blow up so much of the Rajah's force. That part would be up to the brigade, who would give a good account of themselves that night.

A moment later there were brilliant flashes from below, a line of rippling flame as a bombardment started upon the British troops.

Fifteen

The ground outside the wall was harder than Ogilvie had expected; Campbell and the others sweated blood as they dug into it. Hands became torn and blistered as the entrenching tools cut down slowly, too slowly for Ogilvie's impatience. But the wall was almost deserted now, thanks to the strong attack being mounted on the brigade, and was wholly so at the end where the shaft was being sunk; thus there was not the pressing need for silence, not the same compulsion to try to remain hidden. This helped considerably; and inch by inch the shaft went down and the sides were held in place, to Lance-Corporal Campbell's directions, by pieces of wood brought from the commissariat wagons and concealed beneath the Pathan garments. Ogilvie had moved a few paces outward, where he kept a sharp watch for any native patrol. He looked up towards the plateau, where the brigade's mountain guns were in action, countering the heavy guns blasting out from the city outskirts, the guns that would be much too heavy to drag up the sloping ground ahead but which could cause terrible casualties to the British line from where they stood. By comparison, the mountain batteries were little more than popguns, and in spite of their fire the moon showed the fast advance of the Rajah's hordes, both cavalry and infantry.

Ogilvie clenched his fists: Campbell was being bloody slow! When – if – he could reach the magazines, he would at once relieve the pressure on the brigade; time was vital now. His impatience grew as the sounds of digging continued and he went on watching for any signs of a patrol. None came; the attention seemed still to be on the outward thrust of the Rajah's army and on the grenade-shattered gateway where for a certainty there would have been many casualties among the tight-packed Afghans. Ogilvie turned and went back to the lip of the shaft.

As he reached it, Campbell's voice came up.

'Deep enough now, sir!'

'Thank God!'

The infantry battalions waited, holding their rifle fire by Dornoch's order until such time as the enemy was close enough to ensure that every bullet hit home. Ammunition was short, the more so since Ogilvie's party had needed a good deal of powder for their explosive charges and fuse-trails, and there must, Dornoch had insisted, be no waste. In the 114th's sector of the line, the Regimental Sergeant-Major was on the move continually, ensuring that there were no trigger-happy fingers ready to let fly at shadows. In the meantime the bombardment went on and the heavy-calibre shells exploded in front and in rear of the waiting line lying flat on its stomachs. Debris was flung in all directions, chunks of earth and rock missing Cunningham by inches on many occasions. A few of the shells had taken the line fair and square, and the Welch Regiment had suffered some forty casualties. In their sector the doctor and his medical orderlies were fully stretched and torn-off limbs lay in sad disarray. Cunningham had noted that the guns of the mountain batteries were firing with greater accuracy than those of the Rajah: many hits had been scored on the advancing column, which was tending to scatter as a matter of prudence. But the advance continued nevertheless, with a degree of tenacity that Cunningham found worrying: the native levies didn't usually advance in the very teeth of the guns, which tended to induce a certain measure of panic and self-preservation. The attackers didn't appear to be the Pathan element, who would, as ever, be ferociously brave, but Hindu; and by Cunningham's reckoning they were being driven on by an overwhelming sense of purpose and a sureness that their Rajah's vast resources were about to encompass the end of the Raj.

As impatient now as Ogilvie down below, the Regimental Sergeant-Major found it hard to contain his desire to open fire with the rifles and then bawl the Jocks to their feet and charge behind the steel of the bayonets. He turned as the Adjutant came down the line and called out to him.

'Sar'nt-Major...'

'Sir!'

'Orders from Brigade, Sar'nt-Major. The men are to be ready to open very shortly now. If the order is given to charge, the line is to go forward as one. And when they've cut through the enemy, they're to re-form immediately and charge again from the rear. I am passing the orders personally to all Company Commanders. Kindly ensure that the 114th's sector goes forward with precision and determination, Sar'nt-Major.'

'They'll do that, Captain Black, sir.'

'I trust so.' Black rode on. As ever, Cunningham fumed at the Adjutant's supercilious tone and his continual insinuations, not put into words, that the Jocks were going to let the side down in some way.

'Easy now!'

They had cut through beneath the wall and now the second shaft was being driven upwards. Earth and rubble fell around the men's ears in profusion, deepening around their ankles until those behind scrabbled it away to be brought to the surface outside the wall by the rest of the party and scattered clear of the entry to the downward shaft. The ground in the palace garden was soft and the second shaft was in fact nearly through, hence Ogilvie's order to take it easy; the emergence was the danger point and had to be made with care. As the shaft came close to the surface the ground crumbled away and Ogilvie, in the lead of the digging party now, felt the cool of the fresh air. Thrusting an arm up, he found his hand coming free of the earth.

'We're there,' he said. 'Keep silent and keep still till I pass the word to come out.'

Very slowly, very carefully, Ogilvie lifted his head through the lip of the shaft. More earth fell; his mouth, eyes and nose felt full of it. He blinked out into darkness relieved at the far end of the palace grounds by flickering light, the light, he believed, of fires started by the grenades earlier. As half expected, the garden appeared empty of life and after a brief reconnaissance Ogilvie gave the word for his party to emerge. When they were all out he said, 'We advance together through the garden. When we reach the courtyard proper, you'll all remain in cover, keeping to the garden. Lance-Corporal Campbell will see to it that the charges and fuse-trail are laid as soon as I come back with the Major. If I'm not back within half an hour, the command of the party devolves on Sar'nt Wallace who will then have to locate the magazine as best he can, and then carry on as ordered. All right, Sar'nt?'

'All right, sir.'

'Off we go, then. Quiet as you can.'

They moved ahead in file, dark shadows in the night. The moon was still in full sail across the sky but here in the garden there was plenty of cover from its beams. There was still no sign of life, though there was plenty of sound from ahead, sound that grew louder and louder as though tremendous excitement was being generated now that the first move had been made against the Raj.

As the end of the garden came into view, Ogilvie halted his party with orders to wait while he made a brief reconnaissance of the courtyard itself. He went ahead, keeping in cover still. He halted again on the edge of the garden. Men were running about everywhere, waving rifles and *jezails* above their heads, shouting and showing every sign of an almost drunken and frenzied fervour. Fires were still burning in the distance by the gateway, but were tending to die down now as the Rajah's men presumably went into dousing action. A stench of smoke and charred wood lingered on the air.

Ogilvie turned away and went back to his party.

'I've a good chance,' he said. 'I'm not likely to be noticed in the crush, still less recognized as the late messenger of the Amir!

Follow me to the garden fringe, then keep hidden. I'll be back with the Major – if I'm lucky!'

He went ahead again, this time emerging right out into the courtyard. He had been right: no-one took the slightest notice of him, apparently just another Pathan arrived from Afghanistan and waving a British Army-type rifle. He crossed the courtyard towards the great marble steps rising to the main entrance to the palace building itself. At this stage, it was likely that Brora would be at the Rajah's side, intent upon getting back that fake receipt for tainted rupees – or, on the other hand, he could be almost anywhere else, putting into effect his promised inhibition of the Rajah's military potential. But the Rajah himself was the obvious starting point; after that would come the difficulty of attracting Brora's attention without alerting the Rajah. That would have to be taken as it came.

Ogilvie went fast up the steps and into the great hall, where he headed left towards the chamber to which he had been taken for his first meeting with Mohan Singh. He found the place thronged with the Rajah's retinue and concubines, but there was no sign of the Rajah himself or of Brora; the great gold throne stood empty. As he stood by the doorway, searching the crowd, one of the palace retinue waved him angrily away: this hallowed ground was not the place for the Amir's hired banditry, whose task was only to fight and kill the British.

Seeing a need for prudence, Ogilvie turned away and made instead for the staircase leading to the upper apartments. He had no idea where Brora was accommodated and in the event he found nothing; he was not apprehended – as he had half expected, the guards were either on the march towards the brigade's position or were down in the courtyard yelling and rifle-waving with the rest. Worried as to time now, he went down the staircase again at the double, and out into the noise of the courtyard.

Then something came to him: he recalled the prison-like building he had seen during the morning of his sojourn in the palace, the grim barred windows, and the fleeting glimpse of a woman's face: the place where the women destined for the market-place were being held. Brora had got into all this on account of his womanizing or self-confessed whoring. Where there were women, it was likely Brora would be found.

Ogilvie ran fast for the most likely prospect.

'There's more of them than I thought,' Dornoch said. The moon, shining down on the closing natives, showed up what looked like a force of cavalry and infantry some four to five thousand strong, a force that greatly outnumbered the battered British brigade. The hand-to-hand fighting was going to be bloody enough and it was about to start. Dornoch brought up his revolver and aimed it at a tall native whom he took to be one of the Rajah's officers, holding his fire until the wave of men came closer. A moment later he gave the word to open all along the British line, and the bugles rang out, brazen and loud over the rising sound of the attack. Immediately, the rifles and Maxims crashed out and a ripple of flame came from the line. Natives fell in hundreds: there had been no possibility of any of the bullets missing their targets at such close range. But the casualties were not all on the native side; and when the Rajah's force had recovered from the first volley, they came in to close quarters with swords and sabres and scimitars, hacking and slashing and trampling the soldiers beneath the hooves of the cavalry horses. By now, with the two opposing forces inextricably mixed, there was no chance to use the mountain batteries further; they had been brought into action before the rifles opened, but their effect had been limited and they had not deterred the onslaught.

Riding down in rear of the line with the Brigade Major and his orderly officer, Dornoch felt the stab of approaching defeat. Now the natives had broken right through the line: Dornoch laid about with his broadsword, hacking through flesh with a grim determination. Beside him the Brigade Major, with blood running down his face, did the same.

Dornoch called out, 'The flank battalions, Major – the native units–'

'Yes, sir?'

'They'd better be turned. Ride through with orders if you can get there. I'd like them to break from the line and double into positions at right angles to our front, then enfilade the rebels when they re-form.'

'Very good, sir.' Major Calland saluted and spurred his horse forward through the fighting mass, making for the left flank battalion. The orderly officer turned for the right flank. Within moments, Dornoch had lost sight of them both and was engaged in a battle for his life against a heavily bearded native officer wearing a turban in which many jewels sparkled as they were caught by the rifle flashes. This man rode for the Colonel, eyes gleaming, sword-point levelled like a lance. Dornoch brought up his broadsword with the blade held flat to parry the thrust. There was a heavy clash of steel. Nimbly the native officer moved his wrist and brought his sword below Dornoch's and thrust again, but Dornoch moved aside and the steel missed him by little more than an inch. The next thrust took his arm and he felt the run of blood; the two horses collided violently and Dornoch gave a lurch that laid him wide open to the native's sword, but just as the point was aimed at his side the turbaned officer gave a gasp and slumped sideways. Dornoch heard the voice of his Regimental Sergeant-Major.

'Are you all right, sir?'

'Yes, thank you, Sar'nt-Major. Did you do that?'

'Kill the native, sir? Aye, I did!'

There was no time for further exchanges; Cunningham was fighting off all comers with an agility surprising for his years and figure, sweat-soaked but seeming never to tire as he thrust and cut with his highland broadsword. As Dornoch fought through to the front of the British line, he saw that the flank battalions were starting to re-group. He shouted orders, which were taken up by the Company Commanders and NCOs, for the centre battalions to disengage and withdraw back to the original front in an attempt to leave the rebel force exposed to the enfilading fire from the flanks and from the re-grouped centre.

Ogilvie reached the women's quarters, the prison quarters, after passing through the Afghan throng still filling the palace court-yard. He heard sounds from inside the building: the sound of women's voices, raised in fear. Doubling round, he came to a door. There was no guard and the door was neither locked nor bolted. He pushed it open and went inside. He found himself in a passage with a stone floor. Off this passage a door led; currently it was standing ajar. From it Ogilvie heard a voice: Brora's. He hadn't been wrong.

He pushed the door fully open, and Brora turned away from a sea of women's faces. At first he didn't recognize Ogilvie, and lifted an arm to thrust an importunate native un-ceremoniously back. Then he registered;

expressions of surprise and anger crossed the florrid face.

'What the devil! What are you doing here?'

'I've come in with a demolition party to blow the magazine.'

Brora stared. 'The devil you have! D'you mean to kill us all, you fool?'

'No. There'll be a fuse-trail, long enough for us to get clear.' He explained about the tunnel, which with luck should still be available for the escape afterwards; or in the general confusion they might be able to make their getaway through the main gate before the magazine went up. 'There's not much time, Major. Do you know where the magazine is?'

Brora said harshly, 'Yes, I do.'

'Let's get there quick, then.'

'Not so fast,' Brora said. He tapped Ogilvie on the chest. 'I had my own ideas as I think I told you–'

'You didn't say what they were.'

'No? Well, I'll tell you. I have to get that damn receipt back and that comes first. I've not managed that yet. When I have, then I intend to kill that bloody little Rajah, which is all that's needed to stop the rebellion in its tracks, and then get out. And I'm taking the women with me.'

'Because you need to, Major? To do yourself some good later?'

'Yes, if you want to know, damn you!' Brora thrust his face close. 'Fettleworth's going to ask questions, obviously. If I can get the women out – and that receipt back in my hands–'

'You wouldn't have a hope, Major. You're too well known, and if you were seen to be riding out at this stage with the women, you'd be cut down before you'd gone a matter of yards!'

Brora gave a hard laugh. 'You don't know what you're talking about. I have authority here–'

'Only for so long as you're able to keep the Rajah's killing secret. How do you propose to get him on his own, without witnesses?' Ogilvie paused. 'It's got to be the magazine, Major. I'm under orders from Brigade. And in just fifteen minutes from now, Sar'nt Wallace will be looking for the magazine on his own, with orders to blow as soon as he's ready – unless I get back within that time.'

There was no alternative and Brora, albeit grudgingly, saw the sense of Ogilvie's mission. He would not accompany Ogilvie to the magazine; the receipt was vital to him and while the magazine was opened up and the fuse-trail laid, he would be about his final business with the Rajah. He indicated the magazine's whereabouts: it was in a stone-built strong-point adjacent to the perimeter wall on the western side, and it would be guarded by at least two men. Sardonically, Brora wished Ogilvie's party luck. He himself, he said, would get the women to safety before the explosion came, if come it did.

Ogilvie asked how he would get the women out.

'The way I told you,' Brora answered. 'Boldly, through the gate. I shall have an escort.'

'Of what, Major?'

Brora said promptly, 'Afghans! Afghan bandits, the Amir's men whose loyalty is chiefly to themselves rather than to the Amir or his dirty little crony the Rajah – you'll see!'

He would offer no more than that; Ogilvie had to be content. He looked at the faces of the seventy or so women before he left the prison building. Throughout the discussion they had remained mostly silent, almost as though they suspected that the dialogue between the British Major and the Pathan was concerned with their benefit. The eyes, however, had beseeched while the tongues remained still, and the eyes spoke more than words. The hope, the eagerness struck like physical blows; once taken from their homes to pass within the power of Rajah Mohan Singh who owned them body and soul, their lives had virtually come to an end. They were entirely at his disposal; they lived only upon his word and they were available to satisfy his desires when summoned, until the fortunes of his terrible trade took them from the palace to masters who were likely enough to be as bad. And so many of them were young, no more than children by British standards of behaviour; their lives should lie before them, unsullied by such as Mohan Singh. Ogilvie, hoping they could be got out by Brora, detested the knowledge that this might never be. There was much danger; Brora's words had been brave but could prove empty, even though he had a very personal axe to grind in trying to compensate for past errors of judgement, to put it no worse than that; while so far as Ogilvie's help was concerned, the facts were stark and could not be circumvented: the Raj came first.

With the details of the magazine's whereabouts in mind, he lost no more time. Leaving the building, he faded into the shadows behind and made his way back towards the garden. The British party was waiting and Wallace was much relieved to see him back.

'Is all well, sir?' he asked.

Ogilvie nodded. 'So far, yes. We'll need to fight our way into the magazine, but we'll be numerically stronger than the guard. I'm not too worried about that. All set?'

'All set, sir.'

'Right, then we'll move out at once, heading for the western side of the wall. Follow on behind me, and from now on we keep close – except that when we're nearer the magazine I'll carry out a reconnaissance on my own.'

They moved towards the courtyard in a close group with Sergeant Wallace at Ogilvie's side, Corporal MacKendrick bringing up the rear, and Lance-Corporal Campbell taking separate charge of his demolition party, who would go into the magazine as an independent unit, leaving the remainder on guard outside. The fuse-trail would be laid back towards the garden, running close to the wall where it was least likely to be spotted by the defenders of the palace. Once this was lit at the garden end, the whole party would beat it fast for the tunnel. There was still the question of Brora, but Ogilvie felt that that was now in the hands of fate, if Brora allowed fate a chance. The Major was outside Ogilvie's jurisdiction; the Colonel's orders were paramount.

When the magazine was in view, Ogilvie halted his party and moved out alone, cautiously. From beyond the palace walls the heavy guns could still be heard from time to time, firing upon the British brigade.

Sixteen

Moving on, Ogilvie picked up the armed guard, just two men patrolling with their bayonetted rifles at the slope, up and down past a formidable-looking door that stood firmly locked, or at any rate shut. Ogilvie had hoped that perhaps the magazine would be open at this time of action, ready for the issue of arms and ammunition, of grenades and other explosive devices.

No such luck.

As the near-bedlam of hysterical excitement continued in the courtyard Ogilvie crept back towards Wallace and the others.

'It's likely one of the guards will have the key,' he said. 'We'll go in and attack them now. Sar'nt Wallace will lead half the party round the back of the building and then attack from the southern end. Corporals MacKendrick and Campbell will come with me. We'll attack directly from here, and nip the guards in a pincer movement. Split the parties now, Sar'nt Wallace.'

'Aye, sir. Do we shoot to kill, sir, or not?'

'If we have to shoot, we shoot to kill, but I want to avoid attracting any attention – so we'll aim to use the bayonets.'

'And make a quick job of it, sir!'

'That's right, Sar'nt. No screams – go for the throats.'

When the party was split in half, they moved out, Ogilvie holding back for a while to allow Wallace to cover his extra distance round the back and arrive at the southern end of the magazine at the same time as himself.

As bold as brass, as arrogant as ever, Lord Brora stalked into the great chamber leading off the main hall and marched towards the golden throne which was still empty of His

Highness Mohan Singh. Halting, he addressed a cringing man in tones reminiscent of any British parade ground.

'Where the devil's His Highness?'

'Sahib, His Highness is in his private apartments.'

'I see.' Brora turned about and, watched by the assembled concubines who were shortly going to be much disturbed by the explosion if Ogilvie was successful, stalked out of the chamber again and strode across the splendid hall to a corridor leading from its far end. Walking along this corridor, he came to a door guarded by a *sowar* armed with a carbine.

'His Highness,' Brora said briefly.

'Sahib, Highness is not to be–'

'Matter's urgent. Vital! If you don't let me in at once, I'll recommend His Highness to chop your damn head off.'

Visibly shaken, the man stood aside and Brora marched to the door and flung it open. He walked down a short passage, through another door, and into a vast apartment with a thick carpet of peacock blue and deep maroon. Wide windows gave onto the back of the palace where there was comparative peace although the racket from the main courtyard could still be heard in muted form. Across the room, beyond gilded tables and ornate, lacquered cabinets from China and Japan, beyond exquisite paintings upon the richly-hung walls, His Highness could be seen sitting at a great desk of highly expensive tulip-wood. Hearing Brora's approach, he turned.

'Highness, a moment if you please.'

The Rajah's eyes glittered angrily. 'I was not to be disturbed–'

'So I was informed. I doubt if you will be again, so you needn't worry, you filthy little bugger.' There was a curious gleam in Brora's eyes and his face was deeply flushed. 'And get away from that desk.'

'I–'

'Keep your mouth shut. Move away from the desk, God damn you!' Brora, aware that the desk could well hide a means of giving the alarm, moved very fast for a bulky man. He took His Highness by the throat, half strangling him in huge hands, and shook the gross body like a rat. The Rajah's eyes protruded, as did his tongue, and saliva drooled down his face.

'The receipt,' Brora said. He went on shaking. 'You know the one I mean. I'm going to release you now so that you can find it and give it to me. But you're not moving without a little restriction.' He let go with one hand and with the other fished in a pocket of his white suit and brought out an affair of thin wire, looped round its own part and with a wooden toggle for a handle at one end. '*Thuggee*, British fashion,' Brora said. He draped the loop over the Rajah's head and settled it round the neck. 'It's a rabbit snare. Used in England by poachers, not by gentlemen of course, but nevertheless sometimes a handy article.'

He jerked on the handle; the thin wire noose tightened. The Rajah made a strangled sound and tried to run; the wire tightened further, cutting cruelly into the fat neck. His Highness scrabbled at it with his fingers to no avail. Brora laughed. He said, 'Either you'll strangle or cut your neck through if you move again. Now – the receipt, and quickly!'

Approaching the magazine, Ogilvie saw Sergeant Wallace come round the corner of the building just as the patrolling guards, who had spotted nothing untoward so far, turned on their beat and faced the swift advance of apparent Pathans. Wallace and his party were on them before they could react, while Ogilvie led in from his side. The guards never had a chance against the Scots' bayonets, never had a chance even to cry out before the steel went in. The attack was carried out in total silence beyond the pad of the running feet and it was all over within half a minute, with the guards lying in pools of blood that had spread from their throats. Ogilvie ordered the bodies to be dragged round the back of the building, where they were bundled into cover between the magazine itself and the perimeter wall. A quick search revealed the keys; Ogilvie took them and, with Campbell and his demolition party, went fast for the entrance.

Leaving Wallace and the remainder of the Scots on guard with their rifles outside, looking like a part of the Pathan levies detached from the courtyard, Ogilvie unlocked the heavy brass-bound door and went in. He brought out an electric torch fed from a battery inside it, a recent and useful invention. He shone the beam around: the place was primitive, the door opening directly into the magazine itself, an extensive area well stocked with explosives in racks and piled upon the stone floor. Ogilvie recognized British small-arms ammunition in boxes, British shells and British grenades together with the products of many other countries – French, American, Russian, either stolen in raids or bought on the international arms market: barrels of gunpowder – he need not after all have brought his own – thousands of sticks of dynamite, jars of nitro-glycerin unmixed with the kieselguhr that would turn it into dynamite, box after box of fulminate of mercury detonators, and racks of powder charges in leather charge-cases all ready for the big guns. Ogilvie stared at it all, visualizing the result when the magazine went up. It was no small place; it could not be compared with the arsenal at Woolwich, but there wouldn't be much left standing in its vicinity when it blew. He turned to Campbell.

'Right,' he said. 'Lay your charges as fast as you can, then the fuse-trail – right back into the garden as far as the tunnel. How long d'you expect it to take?'

'Can you give me ten minutes in here, sir?'

Ogilvie nodded. It would not, in fact, be necessary to position much in the way of charges; just one to blow the detonators would probably be enough, he believed. When those boxes went, the barrels of powder would follow, then all the rest of the many tons of high explosive. But Campbell was making quite sure: working fast and efficiently, he set his powder charges close to the detonators and around the powder-barrels, with more amongst the dynamite and nitroglycerin. Then, spilling out one of his canvas bags, he began to lay the fuse-trails, one to each of the set charges, all of them leading in to the main fuse that would run from the magazine, through the door, out across the corner of the courtyard, into the dimness of the garden and back to the tunnel beneath the wall, where it would be lit.

He was finished in a little over the ten minutes. He turned to Ogilvie and saluted. 'Charges set, sir, and the fuse-trail ready to be extended.'

Ogilvie nodded. 'Carry on,' he said. As tense now as a violin string, he went for the door while Campbell carefully poured the powder to extend the fuse-trail; outside, all appeared well. Sergeant Wallace reported that no-one had come into the magazine's vicinity. All the attention was still on the continuing battle on the plateau. He had heard shouted orders from time to time and his few words of Pushtu had led him to believe that more men, Pathans this time, would shortly be sent out to help crush the British brigade.

'Let's hope we blow in time, sir,' he said.

Ogilvie gave a tight grin. 'We'll be doing our best.' As Campbell brought his fuse-trail out into the courtyard, the door was brought to but not quite shut: from a casual glance it would appear shut and, at any rate until it was lit, the trail itself was unlikely to be seen. But everything had now to depend on none of the Rajah's army finding a need to visit the magazine before the match was touched to the end of the trail and the lethal spark sped on its destructive journey through the night. As Campbell, bent to his task, backed away and reached the fringe of the garden, Ogilvie ordered the party to withdraw towards the tunnel.

'What about the Major, sir?' Wallace asked.

This was the question Ogilvie would have preferred to have been left unasked. He said, 'The Major has affairs of his own to attend to, and he knows exactly what we're doing. On the other hand–' He broke off, many things revolving in his head. Brora was an arrogant bastard who had got himself into his current situation by his own fault and in so doing had jeopardized the regiment and every man in it, had jeopardized the whole brigade and the safety of the Raj itself. He

288

had asked loud and clear for all he was going to get when the magazine went up. But to leave a brother officer, someone from his own regiment, behind to certain death was rapidly becoming something Ogilvie was unable to face.

He was aware of Wallace staring at him in some concern. He went on. 'He'll have to be found, of course.'

'A needle in a haystack, sir–'

'Yes. But I have to try, Sar'nt.'

'There's no time now, sir. It'll mean delay at best.' Wallace hesitated. 'With respect, sir, the brigade out there is under pressure. And the brigade has to come first, sir. It has to.'

Wallace had been right, of course; as so often on military service, it was the simple question of one life against many, and in all conscience Brora's was an easily expendable one – and, again Ogilvie reminded himself as he withdrew into the garden with the others, he had known the score all along.

Better to forget Brora...

The retreat to the wall and the tunnel seemed endless – painfully slow as Campbell extended the fuse-trail patiently and without allowing the tension and the desire for speed to make him careless. Step by step, moving backwards ... at last they had the wall in sight again and within a few more minutes had reached the vertical shaft that led to safety. Corporal MacKendrick lowered himself into the shaft to check that there had been no fall of earth: he reported the way clear, and swung himself back up again.

'Right,' Ogilvie said. 'All out, and fast. When you get to the other side, run like hell!'

Sergeant Wallace saw the men down the shaft one by one; they didn't linger but it was a slow job all the same. Ogilvie felt his nerves playing him up and he found he was sweating as though from a *chukka* of polo: someone might stumble across that fuse-trail at any moment. Wallace went down behind the others and as the sergeant vanished into the narrow shaft Ogilvie called to Campbell.

'That's it,' he said, and took a deep breath. 'Light the fuse.'

Campbell had his box of Lucifers ready. He took one out, struck it and touched the flame to the powder as he squatted beside it. The fuse-trail began sputtering and sparking away into the night. It moved fast. Ogilvie was counting the seconds now. Campbell moved away, walking back along the powder

290

trail. After a few moments he returned at the double, showing signs of concern.

'What's the matter?' Ogilvie asked.

'It keeps going out, sir—'

'Get back, man, and keep it burning!'

Ogilvie swore. Campbell moved away fast, through the garden towards the courtyard. Clenching his fists, Ogilvie waited: as the officer in command he couldn't leave the palace grounds with one of his men left behind but the wait and tension were difficult to bear at this stage. Campbell had vanished. Straining his eyes through the darkness Ogilvie was unable to pick up any flicker of light that should have come from the fresh match being touched to the powder trail.

A few minutes later a tumult broke out in the courtyard; there were shouts from the distance, shouts that sounded like an alarm being given, cries of panic and some shooting, then the light of flares moving across to the west – towards the wall, towards the magazine?

It was some sixth sense that made Ogilvie dive for the shaft, and he was deep in the linking tunnel below the wall when the whole locality erupted in a colossal explosion that shook the very earth where he lay.

291

His body seemed to rise up, then drop again, and his ears were filled with the thunderous roar as the magazine blew its massive explosive content, a whole series of shattering, violent eruptions that seemed as though they would never end. Nothing would have lived through that. But someone had: as the racket dwindled Ogilvie heard his name called. It was Sergeant Wallace, squeezing down through the outer shaft and laying hold of his outstretched arms, and tugging.

'Captain Ogilvie, sir! Come away, sir! There's nothing left up top, nothing at all.'

It was true, virtually everything had gone and the palace was lying in a smoking, flaming heap of total ruination. There were cries of agony, of despair from inside the remains of the wall. The eastern perimeter was less damaged than the westward part adjacent to the magazine, and this fact had served the Scots as Ogilvie found later. With Wallace's assistance he dragged himself clear of the tunnel, ears and eyes filled with earth, his mind dazed and shaken by the tremendous concussions that had brought the Rajah's dream of conquest to a final end, and must surely have killed him too. With

Wallace Ogilvie moved away from the wall, moved in a hard red light, the light of hell as the fires raged behind him. Great flames shot into the sky, lighting the surrounding country. Ogilvie stared up towards the British-held plateau to the south: the native force could be seen flying in disorder, men streaming to the rear and deserting the fight now that their base had been destroyed and with it their whole reserve strength. The dismal, disorganized retreat was being harried by the brigade, and clear above the sound of the guns and rifles Ogilvie heard the pipes and drums advancing down the slopes, beating out the Royal Strathspey's action tune, Cock o' the North.

'What about Campbell?' he asked.

'Campbell never came out, sir.' Wallace's tone was sombre. 'I can't say what happened in there, sir, but it's my belief Campbell was unable to be sure of getting the fuse relit through to the magazine, so he went in himself to blow the place direct.' He paused. 'If that's the case, sir, then he deserves the Victoria Cross, for he's saved more than the brigade. I dare say—' He broke off, his tone altering. He pointed. 'Now there's something more immediate, sir: the Major!'

'The Major?'

Ogilvie followed Wallace's pointing finger and saw Lord Brora, a distant devilish figure in the red glow from the shattered palace. He was well ahead of Ogilvie's party and he seemed to be waiting, apparently for Ogilvie to catch up, and he had a large number of women with him, huddled together in apparent and natural terror. As Ogilvie came up towards him, his white suit was seen to be torn and bloodied but the gleam of triumph was in his eye and he seemed to be in excellent spirits.

'Good work, Ogilvie – on someone's part,' he said. 'I got out just ahead of it–'

'How, Major?'

Brora laughed. 'I told you, I think, in the palace: with the assistance of the Rajah's hired Pathans, who proved greedier than they were loyal, as I forecast if you remember. I got hold of His Highness' keys, the keys to one of his treasure storerooms.' He gave another loud laugh, an almost crazy sound. 'By God, I came out as the distributor of largesse, Ogilvie, largesse on the grandest scale! I went for the gate, with the women mark you, scattering handfuls of diamonds and rubies and emeralds in such wonderful profusion that the buggers left the gate unguarded in the scramble for wealth, and I was offered no stay, no hindrance – it was too easy! A child could have done it. But I saved the women, Ogilvie.' He sobered down a little. 'Calcutta, I'm sure, will be delighted!'

'No doubt,' Ogilvie said. In some ways it was impossible not to have a degree of admiration for Brora's sheer bravado, but there was a nasty sourness; Ogilvie was thinking of Lance-Corporal Campbell, who had transferred from a safe billet with the Coldstream in Wellington Barracks to find death in the Frontier hills, and who would now never get his commission. Such was the fortune of war, but that was no excuse for Brora. Ogilvie asked, 'Did you bring anything else out, Major?'

Brora took the reference and grinned. 'Yes, indeed I did. I snared the little bugger like a rabbit ... he'll be there still, in bits and pieces. I hoisted him by the neck from one of his own chandeliers after I'd got what I wanted.' His tone became confidential as he took Ogilvie by the arm and led him a little aside, out of earshot of the other ranks. 'All's well that ends well, is it not?'

'You mean–'

'I mean this: there's no reason why certain things should go beyond the regiment. It's never a good thing to–'

'To wash dirty linen in public?'

Brora scowled, looking as if he were about to strike Ogilvie; but he controlled himself. 'Exactly. It reflects upon the regiment. And it's not necessary.'

'Doesn't it depend on the Colonel?'

'He'll see it my way,' Brora said with assurance. 'When I bring the women into Nowshera, rescued by my own hand, I think the good Dornoch will have no damn option!'

He swung away towards the plateau, the fires flickering redly on his broad cheek. He was very much in command of the situation now. With Ogilvie and his party assisting the freed women onwards, Lord Brora led the way towards Brigade through the spiritless hordes of homeless soldiers making their way back to see what could be salvaged from the burning palace.

The brigade was rested through the next day while, below, the palace of Drosh continued to smoulder and send up clouds of drifting black smoke; the place appeared deserted now; the Pathans, or such as were left alive, had already fled back into the hills to bring the message of despair to the Amir in Kabul. There was a good deal of damage to the city itself in those parts near the palace, and details were sent down to assist the townspeople to bring their meagre possessions out from the rubble of their homes. Lord Dornoch rode down himself with an escort to express his sorrow for the inhabitants, his regret at a necessary action. He was met not with hostility but with acclamation: His Highness was well dead and the Raj was glorious.

Next day, before Fettleworth's reinforcements had had time to arrive, the brigade, leaving its dead beneath their cairns of stones and carrying the wounded in the *doolies*, marched out for Nowshera. In due course, after a long march, as the pipes and drums played them into garrison, Bloody Francis, alerted by a mounted runner sent ahead, was there in person to take the salute from his dais and welcome his gallant soldiers back to base. He was beside himself with joy; as he remarked to his Chief of Staff, the whole affair had been handled with the most splendid efficiency and his reports would make glad reading for His Excellency the Viceroy in Calcutta.

'I knew I was right, Lakenham,' he said in an aside as the regiments paraded past with their bloodied bandages.

'In what respect, sir?'

'Why, not to be too hasty with reinforcements, of course. Dornoch – splendid fellow! – he didn't need them after all. It's a lesson for you not to damn well argue with me, I consider. I trust you'll take heed.'

Lakenham ground his teeth in silence. Bloody Francis somehow always contrived to sound as though he were right, and Lakenham thought with weary forebearance of the fulsome and self-congratulatory despatches he would be told to draft for Calcutta. After the regiments had marched past to be dismissed for a stand easy prior to dispersal to their cantonments in Nowshera and Peshawar, the Divisional Commander had words with Lord Dornoch, and with Ogilvie who had organized the final act of victory. But Brora, it seemed, had claimed the General's ear first.

'Your Major, Dornoch,' Bloody Francis said, rasping at his cheek. 'Damn good, I call it – getting all those women out. A brave business altogether, risking his neck inside that dreadful feller's palace. Shows forethought, too. I mean to say ... the man has vision! Getting himself infiltrated ahead – brilliant, really brilliant.' There was a brief silence, then Fettleworth added, 'That

298

document, the one promising Mohan Singh immunity and all that. The usual blasted native chicanery – forged damn signature! Brora knew nothing about it What?'

Dornoch said stiffly, 'That's what Brora told me, at all events, sir.'

'Yes. Quite so. Well, naturally, I'll see that his conduct doesn't go unrewarded, Dornoch, you may be sure. That's all. You may dismiss.'

Salutes were exchanged, and Fettleworth turned away and bounced up the steps into his headquarters, a fat body filled with the self-importance and glory of having saved the Raj. He might get a knighthood out of it; in the meantime he needed a celebratory *chota peg*. As the Divisional Commander vanished into the building, Ogilvie caught the Colonel's eye; each reading the other's thoughts, they turned about and marched back to the battalion.